VENGEANCE
BLIND

A nail-biting suspense thriller

ANNA WILLETT

THE
BOOK
FOLKS

Paperback edition published by

The Book Folks

London, 2018

© Anna Willett

ISBN 978-1-7909-8101-4

www.thebookfolks.com

This book is dedicated to Craig for putting up with me when I'm a million miles away. Thanks for the support and all the cups of tea.

Chapter One

The suitcase, a birthday gift she'd surprised him with only seven months ago, landed on the bed with a leathery thump. Belle listened to Guy's footfalls as he padded back and forth between his side of the walk-in wardrobe and the bed.

"I don't like leaving you like this." His voice was slightly breathless from the hurried packing. "The timing sucks, but what can I do?" She could almost see him raising his broad shoulders in a *what are you gonna do* shrug. If she listened closely, Belle thought she might be able to hear the swish of his silk shirt.

"I'll be fine." She arranged her face into a smile, hoping the effect was relaxed. "Just make sure you have your passport. *And* the script."

She heard the sound of drawers opening and papers shuffling, then she caught the scent of his cologne, its cleanliness with a hint of something floral. As he knelt in front of her, the familiar edges of Guy's face finally came into view. She tried to think of the name of the aftershave, picturing the deep blue bottle that sat alongside his shaving things near the sink.

"You're too good for me." He whispered the familiar words, his lips brushing her cheek and, just for a moment, she wondered if he had any idea how hard this was for her. But the idea was quickly engulfed by guilt.

This was Guy's big break, the chance he'd been longing for and had worked towards most of his adult life. Belle had her success. It was selfish and petty to deny him the same, even if that success had come at the time when she needed him most. She breathed in his scent and leaned into his arms, letting her fingers trace the short hairs on the back of his neck.

"You deserve this." She said the words, knowing it was what he wanted to hear.

His muscles, bunched and tense under her fingers, relaxed and just like that he was on the move again. Hangers rattled as he grabbed clothes and tossed them in the case. She wheeled herself into the bathroom, bumping the door with the edge of her chair. *I'm getting better at doing this blind.* Blind wasn't really the right word; it was more like impaired.

"Hey," Guy called from the bedroom. "What do you need?"

Belle kept moving, waiting for the outline of the vanity to come into focus. "I'm just getting my contacts." She spoke without turning around, determined to stop before running into the cupboard.

"I can do that for you, babe." The kindness in his voice drove home her earlier stab of guilt. He'd been so patient and caring during her recovery, doing everything he could to be there for her. It was wrong of her to resent him for jumping at the job of a lifetime.

The dark edges of the sink fuzzed into view and Belle slowed her progress, coming to a stop just as her toes met with the cupboard. "No need." She ran her hand over the black marble to the left of the sink. Squinting, she spotted the white plastic case. Pleased at being able to do something for herself, she picked up the case and popped open its top. After years of swinging between spectacles and contacts, she didn't need more than the sight she had now to pinch the lens in place.

The bathroom, warmed by the afternoon sun as it fell through a side window, came into focus. With only one eye functioning, her depth of perception was still off, but at least now the world was no longer a haze of colour and shadows. Belle looked up and caught a glimpse of herself in the mirror. Seated in the wheelchair, only her head and shoulders were visible.

She'd been home from hospital almost a week but still hadn't grown used to seeing herself like this: her right eye covered with a patch of thick gauze, tape cutting lines across her swollen cheek and bruised forehead. And her hair… She touched a hand to her cropped hair. It had been her idea for the hairdresser to lop off her long blonde hair.

She let her hand drop into her lap. When Guy arranged for her hairdresser to visit during Belle's time in hospital, she made the snap decision to go from long hair to a short pixie cut. She remembered telling Della what she needed was a transformation. She could almost hear herself, confident, defiant even: *I'm ready for a change.* But the truth was she could scarcely manage to pull herself onto the toilet without help, let alone cope with long greasy, tangled hair.

The bruised and battered reflection of herself looked stark and unfamiliar. Belle didn't see a survivor, just one frightened eye staring out of a gaunt face.

"Okay, babe?" Guy's face in the mirror, tanned and impossibly handsome, was a jarring contrast to the woman she'd become. "I'll wheel you back."

Before she could protest and tell him she could manage by herself, his hands were on the chair, pulling her back with enviable strength. As Belle watched her reflection shirk in the mirror, she couldn't help think she was seeing a replication of what the accident had done to her.

The snapped kneecap, fractured eye socket, and detached retina *had* reduced her. She was no longer Belle Hammer, a successful and respected author, but an invalid. Someone to be cared for, worried about, watched over. She'd never been beautiful, but attractive and curvy. And now... *It won't be forever.* The words repeated in her mind like a mantra, her brain trying to extinguish the flames of despair and depression as they lapped at her consciousness.

"What did you say her name was... the caregiver?" She watched him zip the suitcase and check frantically at his pockets.

"Um... Lea. Lea something." He pulled his phone out and tapped the screen. "Lea Whitehead, a nursing assistant. She'll be here at six." He scratched his chin. "I wish I could wait until she arrives before going, but..."

Belle leaned forward, resisting the urge to clamp a hand to her thigh just above the Velcro cast. Her knee was aching, a deep angry throb that radiated up as far as her hip. "You'll miss your flight. Besides, it's only an hour or so." She pulled her mobile out of the front of her pants and waggled it near her head. "And I've got the phone. Not that I'll need it."

"Here." Guy snatched the phone. "I'm putting Arthur's number in your contacts." He held up a hand, stopping her protests before they could start. "I know you don't like him, but he's harmless and only five minutes away. If you need anything, he'll be more than happy to come over." He held the phone out to her.

Belle hesitated. Arthur Howell's small plot abutted their sprawling ten acres, making him their closest neighbour. While he'd never said or done anything offensive, she couldn't shake her aversion to the man. It wasn't just his waxy skin and shuffling walk that gave her the creeps. There was something about the way he looked at her, the jaundiced whites of his eyes rolling like tobacco-coloured marbles as he watched her movements. There was judgement in the man's eyes, a knowing look suggesting he could see some secret part of her.

"You're right." She took the phone and stuffed it back in her pocket. "I'll call him if anything happens."

Guy's face relaxed. Belle had no intention of calling Arthur, not if the roof collapsed and she was pinned underneath the rubble. But the lie would help Guy feel less guilty about leaving her alone for an hour before the live-in carer arrived. That, she told herself, made being dishonest with the man she loved excusable.

Guy went first. Suitcase in hand, he walked slowly, allowing her to keep pace with him as he made his way through the house. She counted each of his steps: eighteen. When they reached the front door, he set the case down and bent his six-foot frame so their faces were on equal eye level. His lips when they met hers were soft and gentle. Belle let her hands rest on his shoulders, running her fingers over the muscles in his upper arms, muscles he had worked long and hard to build and chisel during hours spent in their home gym.

He pulled back. "I'll call tomorrow. Love you." His lips touched hers once more and then he was opening the door.

"Love you too." Her words made it through the open door a second before it shut.

* * *

The day was fading, weary grey light barely reaching the edges of the couch. Belle wheeled her way to the kitchen. Pausing and straining up with both hands gripped firmly against the chair's armrests to support her weight, she quickly flicked on the sitting room light. She dropped back into the chair with a flop and groaned at the stab in her knee. *I should have asked Guy to put the lights on before he left.* She rolled towards the kitchen, wondering if he'd taken the time to check if the doors were locked. Then, repeating the same awkward manoeuvre with the kitchen light, it occurred to her that Guy should have thought to do these things without being asked.

Just as she'd thought, the backdoor was unlocked. She'd been in the isolated house alone countless times, but being incapacitated added to her sense of vulnerability.

"Damn." Her irritation jumped up a notch as she spun the wheels and crossed the kitchen floor.

Pausing at the window to lean up and flip the curtain aside, she scanned what she could see of the back of the house. From her perspective, only part of the deck and ramp were visible. Without thinking, she counted the bars that were visible on the deck's wooden rail: eight. *There's no one out there.* But still, she strained to see past the deck before letting out a tired breath and locking the door.

She pulled the phone out of her pocket and checked the time. 5:15. Fifteen minutes until her painkillers were due. Would it hurt to take them early? She pulled backwards and turned in a wide arc. The idea of taking the medication and crawling into bed was tempting, but she still had the patio doors to check. Besides, falling into a deep sleep when the nurse was due in forty-five minutes was a bad idea. *No,* she corrected herself. *She's not a nurse. The woman on her way would be more like a babysitter.*

But it wasn't just the need to be alert when the nurse knocked that kept her from taking the painkillers. Part of her didn't want to be asleep as darkness fell. The idea of slumbering in the empty house chilled her. No, it was safer to wait. *Safer.* She almost laughed at the idea of being unsafe. Her writer's brain often made her paranoid. And even though she'd been careful to keep writing out of her thoughts, her mind kept pulling her back to it. She stopped moving and let her hands rest in her lap. Could she still call herself a writer if she hadn't been able to put one word on paper in almost a year? How long had it been since she'd even tried to write?

"I'm not doing this now." She spoke to the empty house, her voice angrier and louder than she expected. It would do no good to work herself into a panic. She'd write again when she was ready. And after the nurse arrived, she'd take her pills and relax.

Just like the back door, the patio entrance was unlocked. Belle swore under her breath and clicked the latch in place. Guy was a kind man but completely clueless when it came to the practicalities of daily life. Something she'd always blamed on his mother. But they'd been married for three years and he'd made little effort to grow up and take more responsibility. She wheeled backwards and headed for the bedroom. Maybe Angela wasn't completely to blame for her son's inability to involve himself in the mundane. *Maybe this is what comes from marrying a younger man.*

* * *

Lea checked the time on the dashboard display. She was supposed to be at Mrs Hammer's house in five minutes, but that wasn't going to happen. Somewhere after leaving Mandurah she'd missed a turn and ended up driving around the old part of Dawesville for almost twenty minutes before getting back on the right road.

"Bloody Google Maps." She reached into the open packet of chips on the passenger seat and grabbed a handful, pushing them into her mouth. Then shaking her salty fingers, she gripped the wheel.

She thought of phoning the woman and letting her know she'd be late, but that would mean pulling over. Her old Barina didn't have Bluetooth and she'd copped a hefty fine for using her phone while driving three weeks ago. The last thing she needed was another four hundred dollar ticket. Not that there was anyone around to see. Lea glanced at the towering gums and tightly packed bush flanking the two-lane road. She'd never been to Lake Stanmore; its isolation surprised her. Nice but a bit of a shock for a city girl.

With the radio turned up, she tapped her fingers on the wheel, burst into song and grabbed another handful of chips. Besides, she'd be there by six-thirty. What difference would half an hour make? She crunched her way through the chips, brushing at crumbs on her pale blue uniform shirt. *Got to cut back on the snacks or someone will be helping me on and off the toilet.*

Still anxious about being late, she glanced at the time on the dashboard: 5:56 p.m. Running late but not by much. Janice at the agency said Mrs Hammer was in her thirties and recovering from a car accident, so it wasn't like she couldn't wait twenty minutes. At least Lea hoped the woman would be all right until she arrived.

According to Google she was approaching Silver Gum Lane. Lea eased off on the accelerator and flicked on the indicator. It was at least ten minutes since she'd seen another car, but old habits... She couldn't remember the rest of the saying, something about being hard.

Lea shrugged and turned onto the side road. Ahead, the narrow strip of bitumen was clear so she leaned over and picked up the cup of Cola from the console and took a slurp. Her eyes bounced back onto the road and widened as something dark fell onto the bitumen.

The Barina's tyres screeched, locking when she stomped the pedal. As the small car began to skid, Lea yelped and released the brake then immediately hit it again just as her dad had taught her to do in emergencies. Heart yammering in her throat, she managed to bring the vehicle to a stop.

"Shit." Her voice was a high-pitched squeal. "Holy shit." She shook her head. Too stunned to be angry, she put the car in park and opened the door.

Whatever the dark outline on the road was, it wasn't moving. The sun was sinking fast, splashing the road with long shadows. Suddenly, Lea wasn't so sure she was doing the right thing getting out of her car to investigate. She glanced back into the Barina and wondered if she should call her father. But he'd been against her taking the job with the agency and calling him for help before she'd even reached her first live-in job would be admitting he was right.

In that moment, torn between diving back into her vehicle or venturing the ten metres or so to check on whatever was crumpled on the road, Lea wondered if her father might have been right when he said it was risky for a young woman to go off to strangers' houses alone. She could almost hear her dad's voice. *I don't care if these people are rich, Lea. Rich doesn't mean they're angels. Who knows what these people are like?*

But the thing on the road had nothing to do with Mrs Hammer or working for the agency, and Lea wanted this job. The money was good and she liked helping people. Being a carer wasn't a glamorous job but it was worthwhile, important. The people she worked with needed someone to help them do things other people took for granted and sometimes they just wanted someone to be there. Most people thought carers just helped people on and off the toilet, but it was much more than that. And, if it panned out, she might even try nursing.

"Okay." Lea let go of the car door. "Hello?" Her voice bounced off the road sounding hollow and frightened. "Are you okay?"

She bit her bottom lip and waited. There was no movement, just the faintest breeze rustling through the leaves in the surrounding forest. *It's probably a branch.* She remembered hearing that gum trees dropped branches without warning.

As she approached, her thick-soled shoes made only the slightest whisper as they moved over the bitumen. Somewhere in the dense bush a bird hawked, the sound reminding her of a baby crying. Now close, she slowed her steps. The details of the dark shape became clear and Lea made a clicking sound with her tongue. A branch, just as she'd thought. A hazard for drivers, but nothing to get all wound up about.

"Jeez." She moved forward, noticing a dip in the air temperature under the shadow of the trees. Shaking her head, she yanked the heavy limb off the road.

Chapter Two

Guy parked the Mercedes on the far side of the long-term parking area. He took his time, making sure to choose a spot away from other cars. With any luck the parking lot wouldn't fill up while he was away. His sports car was less than six months old. The last thing he needed was some idiot putting a ding in the car's sleek black doors and destroying the paint.

He climbed out and unloaded his gear from the boot. He hadn't said anything to Belle, but once his career really took off he planned on buying an apartment in Sydney. Or maybe Los Angeles. The Lake Stanmore house was great, but...

He straightened his sunglasses and slung the leather carry-on over his shoulder. The place at the lake was Belle's. Everything they owned was Belle's. In the dusk light, he checked his reflection in the Mercedes' tinted window. The Armani sunglasses were a good choice for travelling: the gold frames with green lenses were perfect against his tan.

He turned away from the car and headed towards the shuttle. His flight didn't leave for another hour and a half, giving him time to grab a drink in the lounge. He considered checking in, making sure the agency woman had arrived but quickly discarded the idea. Belle would call him if there were any problems. And wasn't she the one that said he deserved this? *Damn right I deserve it.*

What he needed was to relax, read over the script, and get his head in the right space. Belle understood how important this was to him; she wouldn't want him worrying about her. It would be better for both of them if he called her from the hotel. And, after weeks of hospital visits and hanging around the house with nothing to do but wait on his wife, Guy was looking forward to focusing solely on himself.

As he cut across the parking lot his phone vibrated in his pocket. The electronic quiver sent a jolt of anxiety through his chest. It could be Belle or even Andrew, his agent. But somehow he knew it was neither. With a prickle of sweat already gathering on the back of his neck, he let go of the suitcase and pulled out the phone.

Why haven't you called? I need you!!!

"Fuck." He touched his fingertips to his forehead.

He hadn't heard from Katrina in almost two days and was beginning to believe she'd given up. But she was like a nightmare that kept getting worse and all the time gathering momentum. Just when you thought the dream was over, a cold hand grabbed your wrist and yanked you back in. He'd tried reasoning with her but no matter what he said, the girl wouldn't get the message.

The phone vibrated like an angry wasp in his hand, making him jump and almost lose grip of the thing. He cursed under his breath and read the message.

Don't ignore me. I can't stop thinking about you.

He had the urge to drop the phone onto the bitumen and crush it under his heel. Instead, he swiped the beads of sweat off his face with the back of his hand and deleted the messages. He shoved the phone back in his pocket and grabbed his suitcase.

As he trundled past rows of parked cars, Guy saw the shuttle bus pulling away from the stop. "Shit." Now he'd be stuck at the stop for another ten minutes.

When he reached the bus stop, he flopped down on the metal bench. Katrina didn't know Belle's number and the girl had no idea where they lived. At least he hoped she didn't. But then how hard could it be to track someone down? With his mind jumping between what ifs, Guy took off his sunglasses and shoved them in the top pocket of his jacket.

He supposed he could phone her and try to string things out for a while, but then what? She was dangerous and not just because she could go to his wife. The last time he spoke to her, the girl hinted that she was younger than she'd first told him. Something like that could ruin his career before it even started.

Guy leaned forward and rested his elbows on his thighs. How did everything get so fucked up? He couldn't tell Belle. Not with her still recovering from the accident and not unless he was ready to lose her. The only way forward that he could see was to keep ignoring the girl and hope she got tired of the whole thing and moved on to some other poor bastard.

The bus doors hissed open, startling him out of his reverie. Guy stood and grabbed his suitcase. Once he was seated on the shuttle, his nerves evened out and he reached a decision. He'd be in New Zealand for at least two weeks, miles away from Katrina and her crazy shit. Plenty of time for things to cool off.

He leaned back in his seat and caught sight of an aeroplane climbing into the sky. The girl was crazy, but like most nut jobs she would get distracted by something else. The best thing he could do was to sit tight and ignore her. It wasn't much of a plan, but really, what could the girl do? Apart from a few text messages, she had no proof that anything had happened.

* * *

13

It wasn't just the pain anymore. Outside the windows, the sky had almost changed from purple to black. It would be dark in a few minutes and Belle could feel the panic rising, fluttering up from her stomach like a startled moth. The dark frightened her, and the thought of being alone in the dark terrified her. She didn't have the agency's contact details nor did she have a number for the caregiver, Lea. How had she allowed everything to be left in such a muddled state? *Because Guy said he was organising everything and I was stupid enough to believe him.* There was anger now mixed with panic that formed a solid lump in her stomach.

She glanced over at the crutches. She'd practiced on them with the physiotherapist. Six steps one way, six steps back: twelve steps – the irony of the number wasn't lost on her. With the pain in her knee and her face aching, she didn't even want to imagine what it would be like to try hobbling around on her injured leg.

Wheeling through the house in an aimless flurry, Belle heard something that brought her to a jolting stop. A creak. It sounded like someone stepping on a board. She looked up and it occurred to her that while she was locking the back door someone could have entered through the patio doors and crept upstairs. She clamped her hand over her mouth and realised her wrist was shaking.

Was it possible that someone had been in the house with her for the last hour and a half? Scrabbling the phone out of her pocket, Belle called Guy's number. Only half listening to the phone ringing, she kept her eyes trained on the ceiling.

"Come on, Guy." She wasn't sure why she was whispering. If someone had gotten in the house they'd be more than aware of her presence.

After an eternity the call connected. "Guy, it's–"

She was cut off by a robotic voice telling her to leave a message. Hand trembling, Belle tried to think through her next move. She could call her sister, but Bethany and her husband Mark were in Bali, the first time the couple had ventured overseas since the birth of their son Jack two years ago. What good would it do worrying her sister when her sister was so far away? Why hadn't she thought of a contingency plan before Guy left?

Her mind went back to the crutches. Her right leg was fine. If she could make her way out to the garage, she'd be able to drive the car – sort of. Once she was on the road it wouldn't matter where she went. She could pull over somewhere and call the police.

She turned the chair so she was facing the rear of the house. The staircase was out of sight in the dining room. Chewing her thumbnail, Belle focused her attention on the archway leading towards the other room. She'd turned on the kitchen, bedroom, and sitting room light but forgotten the dining room. There had been no more sounds from upstairs. What had she really heard? A creak? Did that mean there was an intruder?

Why would someone go to the trouble of sneaking into the house just to wander around upstairs? If there was a burglar, wouldn't he be trashing the place looking for valuables? She stopped biting her nail and clenched her fists, forcing them into her lap. She had to get herself together. There wasn't anyone upstairs. She was just feeling vulnerable. Unable to run or defend herself, almost blind without her contact, there was nothing that could hurt her, not in her own home.

But if that was true, why couldn't she make herself move? If there was nothing to fear she'd be able to wheel through the dining room and take a look at the foot of the stairs. Her thumb was in her mouth again; this time she used her teeth to tug at the skin around the nail.

She heard a noise and twisted in the chair, frantic to track the sound. Her patched eye, like a black glove on her face, obscured her vision. It took her a few seconds to recognise the hiss of tyres on the driveway and turn the chair around.

Lights spilled through the front windows momentarily flooding the sitting room with yellow light. It had to be the caregiver. Belle pushed forward, skimming across the room and coming to a stop beside the window. Still edgy but no longer shaky, she tipped a slat on the blind. The glare from the car's headlights was too dazzling. For a second Belle could make out little more than the shape of a vehicle before the engine cut and an outline became visible.

The outside sensor lights sprang on and the outline became an easily definable female shape. Belle let go of the blind and pulled back from the window. The panic she'd felt only a minute before was ebbing, leaving her limp with relief and a little embarrassed.

She ran a hand through her hair and straightened her top. She could feel damp patches of sweat under her arms from all the racing around. When the carer knocked, Belle took a quick sniff at her armpit. Satisfied that she didn't smell like an old sports sock she opened the door.

After the initial greetings, Belle asked the young woman to take a seat on the couch. Sitting facing each other, there was a moment of silence.

"I'm so sorry I'm late." Lea sat forward almost ready to topple off the couch. "There was a problem on the road… It sort of held me up for a while."

Alone and waiting for the girl to arrive, Belle had felt an almost overwhelming sense of anger and resentment, but now with the young woman smiling and apologetic all she could do was nod. "That's fine." She waved a hand in the air. "It was no big deal. I'm just glad you made it safely. So what sort of trouble did you have?"

The girl's face was blank as though confused.

"You said there was a problem on the road." Belle didn't want to push, but the carer was almost an hour late.

"Oh." She gave a slight shake of her head. "Yes, sorry. There was something blocking the road and I had to stop and get out to move it. Then…" Lea hesitated, staring down at the coffee table. "Then I thought I saw someone."

Belle's still jumpy nerves twanged at the idea of someone lurking on the quiet roads. "Who?" She realised her voice was too loud, but the girl didn't seem to notice.

"No one." Lea looked up. Her blue eyes flittered between Belle's face and the coffee table. "I mean I *thought* I saw someone, but it was just the shadows." She chuckled. "I guess I'm too much of a city girl. The empty roads sort of freak me out."

Belle felt a stab of sympathy for the young woman. It couldn't be easy coming into a strange home and not knowing anything about the person she'd be looking after, not to mention the isolated setting. Belle of all people could understand how unsettling it could be.

"Well, don't worry about all that now. You're here and that's the main thing."

Lea nodded, but still looked a little unsure.

"Um... Do you want to take your bag up to your room? I'd come up with you..." Belle tapped the arm of her wheelchair. "But as you can see, stairs are not my friend at the moment."

"Oh, yeah." Lea stared at the chair as if she'd only just realised Belle was sitting on it. "No problem. Just point me in the right direction."

Belle showed Lea through to the sitting room. Once they were at the foot of the stairs, Belle rolled to a slow stop. Looking up the steep curving stairway, Belle remembered the creaking sound that got her so worked up and wasn't sure she wanted to send the girl up alone.

"Your bedroom's up there." Belle point to the steps. "It's the first door on your right. There's a TV in your bedroom, but you won't get many channels out here." Belle was stretching the moment out, trying to find a way of warning Lea before sending her up. "There's a bathroom up there and another bedroom, but my husband uses it as a gym. There's the laundry." She pointed to the open doorway on the right of the stairs. "There's extra towels and blankets in there if you need them."

Lea picked up her small pink suitcase and headed for the stairs. "Okay, thanks."

"Wait."

The girl had one foot on the stairs when she stopped her.

"Look, this is a bit awkward, but..." Belle touched the back of her neck, forgetting that she no longer had long hair to fiddle with. "I thought I heard a noise up there earlier." The last sentence came out in a rush.

Lea looked up at the ceiling. "What sort of noise?" She sounded calm and unconcerned, making Belle feel like a frightened child.

"It's nothing, just a creaking board. Probably the house settling, but…" She trailed off, not sure how to finish the thought.

Lea looked down, meeting Belle's gaze. "Don't worry, Mrs Hammer. I'll have a look around." The girl's voice was sombre and reassuring.

Belle listened, counting the girl's footfalls as they grew fainter. Fourteen steps to reach the second story. A door opened, then more creaks as Lea moved around overhead. Belle cocked her head to the side and began counting. She could have pulled out her phone and timed the girl's progress, but there was something comforting about mentally ticking off the seconds. Thirty seconds and then another door opened. *She's in the bathroom.*

This time Belle only reached seven seconds before Lea was on the move again. She heard the girl open another door. Belle recognised the wheezing creak that came from the smaller room at the other side of the house. Counting off the seconds in her head, Belle waited. She made it as far as forty before a soft thud halted her progress.

"Lea?" Belle pulled closer to the stairs. "Is everything okay?" Her voice echoed up the wooden staircase. When there was no response she tried again. "Lea, what's going on up there?" She could hear fear creeping into her voice.

Chapter Three

After a few seconds with no answer, Belle ran a hand over her mouth and looked around the dining room as though hoping help would appear. Her gaze landed on the patio doors, the glass blank like frozen ice on a black pond. Had someone come in through the door after Guy left?

She shouldn't have let the girl go up there alone. What was she thinking? "Lea?" Half out of her chair, balancing on one foot, she was close to screaming.

"Yes?" The girl's head appeared around the curve at the top of the stairs, suggesting she was on her way down and stooped to answer.

Belle staggered to the right, her good leg almost collapsing under her weight. A flood of darkness clouded her eye and the dining room tilted.

"Mrs Hammer." Lea's arm was under Belle's. Supporting her with surprising strength, the girl helped Belle back into the chair. "Are you okay?"

Dark blue eyes swam in front of Belle's face. She opened her mouth to answer, but couldn't catch her breath. Instead, she shook her head, struggling to hold back the tears that were twisting the back of her throat.

"It's okay." Lea was behind her, pushing the chair. She thought of asking where she was taking her, but the effort of speaking seemed too much.

"Now." Lea parked the chair next to the couch. "I'm going to help you onto the couch and then make you a cup of tea. Have you eaten?" Before Belle had a chance to answer, the girl slipped her arms under Belle's and was pulling her out of the chair.

The lift was awkward. At one point too much weight landed on Belle's left leg and she cried out in pain and surprise. "There you are," Lea said as she plopped her onto the couch.

Without waiting to be asked she took hold of Belle's ankles and swung them up, turning her sideways. "Now you just stay there and I'll sort you out something to eat."

Leg pulsing and head aching, Belle slumped back on the couch and watched Lea disappear through the archway. Belle didn't want tea; she wanted her pills. She wanted the endless day to end. But most of all she wanted a drink.

It had been just over a year since her last drink. Almost thirteen months. Long arduous months. At the beginning each day felt like a marathon of craving and denial. Wanting a drink, but telling herself she wasn't an alcoholic. Alcoholics were incapable of work, unable to function and maintain relationships. She wasn't one of those people. Belle was a successful author and happily married. She drank, that's all. No big deal.

But then the denial would turn into panic when her brain and suddenly her body were screaming for a drink, her mind rationalising the need for alcohol. *I work hard. It helps me unwind. I just need something to take the edge off.* Then back to a state of panic where she couldn't hide from the truth. The torturous cycle all before noon left her physically exhausted and irritable to the point of rage.

"Here you go." Lea set down the tray with enough force to rattle the cups. "I've made us some toasted sandwiches and tea."

She put a plate on Belle's lap then settled herself in the armchair. One leg tucked under her, she bit into her sandwich. Belle looked down at the toasted bread but didn't pick it up.

"Thanks for the food, but I really should have my tablets. I was supposed to take them almost two hours ago and… Well, my leg hurts."

Lea's expression remained unchanged as she chewed and swallowed. For a moment it seemed she wasn't going to answer. "It's after eight." She spoke around a mouthful of food. "Better for you to eat first then you can have your medication and go to bed."

Belle frowned. There was a flat certainty in the girl's voice that suggested the topic wasn't up for discussion. Belle felt a tingle of irritation. The caregiver was here to assist her, not set out a routine. But if she argued with the girl, things might get uncomfortable. Did she really want to cause a problem on the first night? And, what if Lea decided she didn't like Belle's attitude and left? The idea of spending the night alone was more daunting than enduring another ten minutes of pain.

Belle nodded and picked up the sandwich. She wasn't really hungry, but the sooner the meal was finished the sooner she'd get her pills. It briefly occurred to her that she was substituting the pills for alcohol, but she dismissed the idea, telling herself the tablets were prescribed for pain. When the pain went, so would her need for the medication.

While Belle slowly plodded her way through half a sandwich, Lea wolfed down her food and disappeared upstairs. As the minutes dragged by, the ache in Belle's leg grew into a throb. The girl's trip to the bathroom added another five minutes to the wait for her medication and Belle could feel her skin growing hot with impatience.

Once the carer returned and they were in the bedroom, Lea began turning down the bed. When Belle wheeled herself out of the bathroom, the bedroom was a blur. She counted the pushes, four to reach the side of the bed.

"Lea, would you hand me my glasses." Belle held out her hand in what she hoped was the caregiver's direction.

"Okay." Lea's voice beside her was an unexpected shock. "Once I get you into bed."

"No, I can't see with–"

Without warning, strong arms snaked under Belle's armpits, pulling her up and forward. She winced at the jarring pain in her leg and gave an awkward hop.

"That's it, you're doing fine." Lea's voice blew past Belle's cheek in a wash of hot air.

Belle grasped the girl's shoulders. She felt off balance and was unable to make out the outline of the bed. She felt like a sack being hauled unceremoniously onto the mattress. Landing with a groan, Belle clutched the bed desperate for something solid to cling to.

"Here you go." Lea slapped the spectacles into Belle's palm. "Where are your pills?" There was no trace of exertion in the carer's voice.

Still reeling from the shock of being jerked out of her chair and dumped on the bed, Belle was unable to speak. Glasses clamped in her hand, she clutched her thigh and sucked in a laboured breath. It was too much. Whether or not Lea realised it, she was over-stepping her role. Her approach wasn't like anything Belle had experienced in the hospital. There was nothing she could do now, but in the morning she'd get the agency details from Guy and ask them to send a replacement.

Hand trembling, Belle pulled her glasses on. Because of the thick padding over her injured eye, the lens was askew, but at least she could see her surroundings.

Still breathing heavily, she nodded to the chest of drawers. "Over there, the Troplozine."

Belle leaned her head back on the pillows and watched the girl cross the room, noticing she was limping. The hitch in Lea's gait was slight, but more noticeable when she turned. She wondered if the girl had hurt herself trying to lift her. Belle felt a stab of guilt. She'd been so focused on her own pain and discomfort that it hadn't occurred to her that Lea was doing her best and maybe struggling.

"Lea," Belle pulled herself up in the bed. "Are you all right?"

The caregiver set the pill bottle down next to the bedside lamp. "Yes, I'm fine. I'll just get you a glass of water."

"But you're limping." Belle hesitated. "Are you... Did you hurt yourself lifting me?"

When she turned from the door, Belle had the distinct impression the girl was angry. Something about her posture and the set of her jaw hinted at tension. But, with misaligned perception, it could have been more about Belle's vision than what the girl was doing.

"No. Nothing like that." Lea bent and lifted the right leg of her pants. "It's just this." She tapped the prosthetic. "When I'm tired my limp's more noticeable."

Belle could feel the heat creeping up her neck. She'd put Lea on the spot, embarrassed her. No, worse than that; she'd pushed the carer into revealing something personal and most likely painful.

"I'm sorry. I didn't mean to... I shouldn't have asked." She was stumbling, trying to find the words but the apology came off as clumsy.

As Belle floundered, Lea leaned on the doorframe, her posture relaxed. "Don't worry, it's just one of those things." Her voice was tight, suggesting she was holding back her emotions. "I lost my foot in an accident a couple of years ago." She crossed her arms. "I don't usually talk about it. It makes people..." She looked up, seeming to inspect the ceiling. "Uncomfortable." For a second neither of them spoke, then Lea broke the awkward silence. "I'll get you the water."

Alone in the bedroom, Belle closed her eyes. She'd been wrapped up in her pain, complaining about her knee and demanding her pills: neurotic to the point of making the girl search the house in case the bogeyman was hiding upstairs. To someone like Lea, she must have sounded like a spoiled child. She ran her fingers through her hair. *I am spoiled. Spoiled and self-involved.*

Belle pulled the phone out of her pocket and put it on the bedside table. She'd actually considered ringing the agency because she didn't like the way Lea lifted her. Just thinking about it made her cringe with embarrassment. *There I go thinking about myself again.*

"Here you go." Lea held a glass of water. "I'll put this next to your bed."

Belle nodded, unsure if she should broach the subject of the girl's accident. Maybe it was a way for them to find common ground. After all, they'd both been injured. Lea worse than Belle, but still it could be a good place to start.

"All right." Lea handed Belle the pill bottle.

She was supposed to take two, but Belle shook three tablets into her palm and tossed them into her mouth. If Lea noticed she'd taken an extra tablet, she said nothing.

Lea picked up Belle's phone. "I'm putting my number in here. That way if you need me in the night you can give me a buzz."

"Thank you." Belle pulled the covers up around her chest, lying back, grateful that the day was almost over. It would be better, she decided, to talk tomorrow. Make the new day a fresh start and see if they could have a pleasant fortnight together.

"Do you want the lamp left on?" Lea's voice sounded distant, like an echo.

Belle nodded and pulled her glasses off. The last thing she saw before the room became a haze was the carer's face. Cool blue eyes like a cloudless sky regarded her with great interest.

Chapter Four

Guy stretched his back and tossed his bag on the bed. After a seven-and-a-half hour flight, he needed to move, get his blood pumping and his limbs loose. The studio paid for him to fly business class, a sign that he was important to them. Valuable enough for them to start spending big money on him. They hadn't sent anyone to meet him at the airport, but it was the middle of the night.

Shrugging off the idea that he wasn't receiving the full star treatment, he focused on the positives. No one ever made it in movies without believing in themselves. Business class flights, five-star hotel; he was on his way. And this time he wasn't depending on Belle to foot the bill. He loved his wife, but couldn't suppress a wave of satisfaction at finally earning some recognition. *I deserve this.* He liked the sound of those words.

But, despite the luxury and the sense of success, he still couldn't shake the feeling of being restricted. Restricted and edgy. He checked his watch: almost 4 a.m. The hotel gym would be open and deserted, making it the ideal time for a workout.

Five minutes later he had his training gear on and was ready to go. His phone sat on the bedside table. He hadn't bothered to turn it back on after the flight. Guy twisted his wedding ring, turning it like a screw on his finger. The studio might have sent someone and he missed them because his phone was off. In the movie business you never turned your phone off, not even at a funeral.

"Fuck." He strode over to the bedside table and grabbed his mobile, turning it on with an impatient stab. "How bad can it be?"

He gulped in a shaky breath. There were six messages. One from Jason Critchen at the studio, the others were all from the same caller.

Why are you being like this? I love you, but you cut me out.

Guy deleted the first message and then the next three without reading them. When he got to the last one, the strength went out of his legs and he sat down on the bed.

You're making me do something you'll be sorry for. I didn't want it to come to this, but maybe once you see the damage I can do you'll be desperate to talk to me.

He held the phone like it was a poisonous spider, the touch of the cold plastic setting his teeth on edge. Katrina was crazy. If he'd had any doubts, the last message made it crystal clear. Part of him knew it was dangerous getting involved with someone like her. But she was so attractive, almost dazzling. Not because of her good looks, although she was pretty. But it was the flaws that got him every time. Katrina was damaged and he couldn't resist a woman with an edge. Wasn't that what drew him to Belle?

Guy tossed the phone on the bedside table and flopped back on the bed. He didn't want to think about his wife, but her image filled his mind. Not of Belle at home pushing herself around the house like a ghost, but the woman he'd first met in the early hours of morning in a hotel in Mexico.

He turned his head and watched the city lights through the floor-to-ceiling hotel window. But he wasn't seeing the night sky, Guy was watching Belle powering through the water, a lone figure in the hotel pool. He sat on a lounger, the slippery fabric damp and clinging from the humidity. Still mildly drunk from the wrap party, he stayed in the shadows, a half-full bottle of champagne at his feet.

When she'd finished swimming, Belle climbed out of the pool. He was struck by the colour of her skin, like caramel in the moonlight. She wore a one-piece suit, sensible and functional, nothing like the skimpy little things most women wore.

He must have nudged the bottle with his foot, because it tipped and clanked on the paving, the sound shattering the silence and drawing Belle's attention. Her head snapped in his direction and she immediately picked up her towel and wrapped it around her body. There was something modest in her reaction that was surprising and alluring at the same time.

He watched her walk around the pool. She had a cautious way of moving, but it was only when she stopped at a lounger and picked up her glasses that he realised she might have been moving with uncertainty because she couldn't see clearly. With her glasses in place, he caught her glancing his way and gave her a smile. Even under the moody pool lights, he could see she was flustered. Her shyness only made her more appealing.

"Are you a swimmer?" It was the first thing that sprang to mind. Not a great pick-up line, but enough to get her attention.

"What?" She pushed her glasses up on her nose and looked at him with confusion creasing her brow.

It was the opportunity he needed, an excuse to move closer. Guy picked up the champagne bottle and crossed to where she stood. "I just noticed you swimming. You make it look easy so I thought maybe you were an extra on the movie."

Her confusion softened into a smile that was warm and somehow vulnerable at the same time. His heart did a weird flip-flop and the bottle almost slipped from his hand.

"No." She shook her head and a spray of water dappled his shirt. "Oh, no. I've got you wet." She said the words with such innocence that Guy couldn't help laughing.

Five minutes later they were chatting about nothing important. She wasn't beautiful. She was pretty, but not flawless in the way most actresses were. She had a charm that came from a combination of intelligence, good humour, and unpretentiousness. And there were her flaws. She was self-conscious, too curvy to be considered slim and too short to be thought of as striking. It stirred something in him that he couldn't quite identify. Maybe he'd strived so long and hard for physical perfection, he needed a woman who was real, tangible. Whatever the reason, he wanted Belle from those first few moments. They spent the next week together and six months later they were married.

Guy pulled his gaze away from the hotel window. Now three and a half years later he was cheating on her with girls like Katrina. He pulled himself off the bed and went to the mini bar. He wanted a beer but wouldn't risk looking bloated on the first day of shooting. Instead, he grabbed a tiny bottle of vodka and drank it with the fridge door still open.

Things had gone wrong somewhere along the way. No, he corrected himself. Not somewhere along the way. He knew exactly when he started filling the void in his life. He tossed the empty bottle at the waste-paper basket and missed. He pulled out another bottle, this one whiskey. Rubbing his eyes, he drained the mini and underarmed it into the bin. He couldn't let himself think about the past. Not now. Not with Katrina to worry about.

By the time he'd downed the fourth mini, Guy felt mellow. The tension had drained from his shoulders and all thoughts of the gym were swallowed by the need for sleep. He'd worry about Katrina tomorrow. She was nuts, that was clear. The messages were over the top, but how far was she really willing to go?

He pulled off his shoes then stripped down to his underwear. Ignoring her was probably the best course of action. His head landed on the pillow and a few seconds later he was asleep.

Chapter Five

"Mrs Hammer." The words jolted Belle awake.

A circle of light surrounded Lea's head. The girl's face was only inches from Belle's. Lea's eyes and features were almost clear when she got this close.

Still fuzzy from sleep, Belle tried to reconcile what was happening. "What? What's wrong?" Her tongue felt thick like it was dry and enlarged.

"I thought you called me?" Lea pulled back slightly and her face took on blurry edges. "I was asleep. I heard something." The words came out in a rush. "It wasn't you?"

Belle's heart fluttered uncomfortably. "No. No, I didn't call. What did you hear?" She was fully awake now, pulling herself up in the bed and reaching for her glasses.

"I'm not sure." Lea spoke slowly, stringing out the last word. Belle could see her clearly now and noticed she was wearing oversized pyjamas. "It might have come from out the back." She jerked her thumb towards the door. "I'd better go and take a look."

"No." It came out as a shriek, louder than she intended. Belle took a breath and tried again. "I mean, it's not a good idea for you to go outside alone." She swallowed, remembering the uneasy feeling she'd had after Guy left. She'd felt certain someone was in the house. Maybe her instincts had been correct.

Lea leaned down and patted Belle's hand. "I'm sure it's nothing. I'll just take a quick look around." She sounded confident, but Belle noticed the way she glanced at the bedroom door. Lea was worried, maybe even scared, but doing her best to stay calm.

"I'll come with you." Belle threw back the covers. Going outside in the dark was the last thing she wanted to do, but she couldn't just sit there while Lea went into the night alone.

"No." The girl held up her hand. "It will be quicker and easier if I go alone."

She was right. Belle would be a hindrance, not to mention the time it would take to get her out of bed and in the chair. It made sense for Lea to go alone. And a small part of Belle was relieved she didn't have to venture outside. However, going alone seemed foolhardy.

"Don't go out there." Belle snatched up her phone. "I'll call the police and… and we'll just wait until they arrive."

She saw something flicker across Lea's face in the shadowy light: impatience or maybe even disgust.

"And what will you tell the cops? I heard something go bump in the night?" There was contempt in the way she spoke, her tone so harsh it made Belle pull back in the bed. "No." Lea spoke with finality. "Just wait here."

"All right." Belle kept her voice even. "But make sure you have your phone with you."

Lea nodded, but it was an absentminded gesture, suggesting she was only half listening. A second later she was gone and Belle was left alone. She fell back into counting, a habit that was familiar and comforting. Thirteen seconds later the back door rattled.

Belle looked down at her phone. 4:08 a.m. How long would it take her to look around outside? The pool area and the deck would be easy to check if she put the outside lights on. But the property stretched for acres. If someone was lurking in the trees, it would be almost impossible to spot them. *Lurking in the trees.* The idea made her breathless.

She thought of getting in her chair, but noticed Lea had parked it out of reach near the bathroom door. Despite the anxiety over a possible prowler, Belle felt a jab of annoyance. Why had the caregiver parked her chair so far away? What if she needed the toilet?

"Damn." Lea was out in the dark making sure they were safe and Belle still managed to worry about her own needs. "What the hell is wrong with me?"

She glanced at the phone noticing it was now 4:12 a.m. Belle made a decision. If Lea wasn't back in ten minutes, she'd call the police. So what if she looked like an idiot? It wasn't like the neighbours would see the police car pulling up in the middle of the night. And then a thought crystallised in her mind with frightening clarity.

Arthur, their nearest neighbour. Guy put his number in her phone in case she needed him. What if Guy told the man he was going away? Guy could never see it, but Arthur was strange. Strange and creepy. If he knew she was alone with the carer, maybe he was the one hanging around. What if *he* had slipped into the house earlier and hid until they were asleep? The noise Lea heard could have been Arthur moving around the house.

The idea of her neighbour sneaking around the house while they slept made Belle's stomach clench. She looked around the room almost expecting to see the man folded behind the curtains. She bit down on her thumbnail, hating the torturous waiting. If only Lea had left the chair near the bed, at least then Belle would be able to get to the kitchen.

"Damn it, Lea." Even as she cursed the caregiver, she wished for the slam of the back door to signal her return.

Her thumbnail was ragged when she pulled it out of her mouth and checked the time. 4:19 a.m. Three more minutes and she'd call triple zero. She glanced at the wheelchair. Three, maybe four hops would do it. Sandy the physiotherapist made her walk twelve steps on the crutches. Could a few hops be that much harder? But without her knee cast for support, Belle had no idea if she could make it across the room.

Despite the chill in the air, Belle was sweating. She could feel the moisture on her back clinging to the thick cotton sweatshirt. *When did I become so helpless?* The easy answer was when a car came out of nowhere and rammed her off the road. But it was more than just the accident, although that played a part. Losing her ability to see and walk left her confidence in tatters. A small voice inside her said otherwise. The voice wanted her to believe she could only be confident and fearless when she had a few glasses of wine under her belt.

The back door clanged and Belle let out a huff of air. "Lea?" Instead of the carer's voice, Belle heard only footsteps. "Lea?" She repeated the name and this time there was a desperate edge to her voice.

A shadow fell across the floor and Lea appeared. "Yes?" She strode across the room, her baggy green pyjamas flapping as she moved.

"Damn it, Lea." Belle slammed her palm on the bed. Her frazzled nerves were stretched so thin, her mind was jumping. "Why didn't you answer me?"

Lea kept moving, grabbing the curtains and pulling them open. "I didn't hear you." The girl's long dark ponytail swayed as she turned her head back and forth as though watching something.

"What is it? Was there someone out there?" Belle was on the edge of the bed now, her good leg over the side, ready to hop.

"Yes." Lea shook her head but didn't turn around. "I mean no. I didn't see anyone, but…"

"But what? What did you see?" Belle's hand was in her hair, pulling it into wild spikes. "What's going on?" Her voice was rising, reaching an almost hysterical pitch. She couldn't take much more; her nerves were as jagged as her fingernails.

"Nothing." Lea looked over her shoulder. "I just meant that if there was someone there, I didn't find them." She closed the curtains, shutting out the night and walked to the bed.

Her explanation had done little to calm Belle's anxiety. Still holding the phone, she was weighing up the idea of calling the police. If she said there was a suspected prowler, they'd have to come and check it out. That might be enough to scare Arthur away. *If it is Arthur.*

"Do you want to use the bathroom before going back to bed?"

Ten minutes later Belle was back in bed, but any chance of sleep had evaporated. She lay back on the pillows and watched Lea turn off the bathroom light then settle the covers around her as though she were a child. She wanted to tell the girl she was capable of pulling up the doona, but bit back the words.

"Okay." Lea scanned the room. "That's everything. I'm going back to bed. If you need me, give me a buzz."

Belle still had her glasses on. Taking them off made her more vulnerable and she wasn't totally convinced they were safe. "Before you go, would you put my chair where I can reach it?" She hoped her voice sounded casual without a trace of reprimand.

"Why?" Lea's face was placid, but Belle thought she detected a hint of annoyance.

For a moment neither spoke until the silence stretched to the point where Belle couldn't stand it anymore. "Because I'm asking you to."

Lea's head came up and angled to the left. Her blue eyes looked less like a cloudless sky and more like a dark pond. For an instant Belle thought the girl would refuse, but instead she gave a slight shrug and brought the chair over, letting the wheels bump against the bedside table.

As the caregiver stood beside the bed, Belle noticed she was wearing sneakers. "Where did you look?" She'd meant to ask the girl when she came back into the house but had been side-tracked by the way Lea rushed to the window. It was the sneakers that prompted her memory.

"What?" Lea frowned and Belle noticed the girl's eyebrows drew together like furious wings.

Belle spoke slowly, drawing out the words. "When you went outside, where did you look?" She knew she was being condescending, but couldn't stop herself. As petty as it was, she felt like she was wrestling back some control over the situation.

"I checked the deck then looked around the lawn." She reached back and ran a hand down the length of her ponytail. "I had a look near the trees on the right of the house, but I couldn't see anything. Why?"

Belle didn't know Lea well enough to know if the girl was telling the truth. *Why would she lie?* Belle had no idea why Lea would lie about checking outside, but something in the girl's posture, maybe her shifting gaze or the way she played with her hair, gave Belle pause. If she had lied about checking outside, was she lying about hearing a noise? It made no sense for the carer to make up such a story. Suddenly, Belle wanted the girl out of her house.

"Okay." Belle pulled off her glasses. "Good night, Lea."

Chapter Six

Lea sat at the kitchen table, her toast smothered in vegemite and heaped with avocado. She ate with enthusiasm, munching through her breakfast with the appetite and urgency of one who had just completed a marathon. Belle couldn't help wondering how the girl remained so trim with such a hearty appetite.

"You're not eating." Lea spoke around a mouthful, not bothering to swallow before speaking.

Belle sipped her tea without answering. Lea wore a navy shirt and pants almost identical to the outfit she'd had on the day before. Or maybe it was the same ill-fitting garb, only today she'd dressed the uniform up with a pale blue scarf wrapped around her neck and knotted at the throat. The morning sun, though weak, made the previous night's drama seem like a lifetime ago. Some of the uneasiness she felt during the night had passed, but there was still something about the caregiver that bothered Belle.

Lea wiped her mouth with the back of her hand. "After breakfast I'll help you to shower."

"No." She sounded abrupt, but no longer cared. The last thing she wanted was for Lea to undress her and watch her struggle naked onto the shower seat. The thought of the slim young woman staring at her soft muscles and almost forty-year-old skin made Belle cringe. "Just help me onto the shower seat and I'll do the rest."

Lea dropped a corner of crust onto her plate. "If you slip, you'll–"

"If I slip, call an ambulance." Belle pushed away from the table and turned the chair in a tight circle. "I'll get my things ready and meet you in the bathroom."

By the time she reached the bedroom, she was panting. It had been almost a month since the accident, a month since she'd been able to swim her daily laps. How quickly her fitness had ebbed and her muscles had turned soft. But as the doctors were fond of telling her, it will take time. She pulled open the dresser drawer and snatched out clean underwear and a dark cotton tracksuit. *Now that I can't write, all I have is time.*

With everything she needed, Belle moved into the bathroom. She'd made a decision while chasing sleep in the early hours: Lea had to go. As much as she'd hoped they'd find common ground, last night was the final straw. The girl was strange – emotionless and bossy. And, while her attitude bothered Belle, she could probably put up with her for a few weeks if not for the sense that Lea was dishonest. She pulled the phone out of her pocket and placed it next to the sink. Once she was showered and dressed she'd ring Guy and have him give her the agency's number.

He'd think she was paranoid, maybe even try to talk her out of calling the agency. *He's not the one stuck in a wheelchair.* It was a bitter thought, one that surprised her with its intensity. He hadn't called. Maybe her dissatisfaction with Lea was amplified because she was angry with Guy. Angry because he left her alone when she needed him most *and* because he hadn't called.

She rubbed the area over her injured eye, her fingers moving over the fading yellow bruise. "I'm angry at myself."

"What did you say?"

Lea's voice behind her was a surprise. Belle's head snapped up, catching sight of the girl reflected in a nearby mirror. "I... nothing." Belle shook her head. "Just thinking out loud."

Lea held Belle's gaze in the mirror before letting her cool blue eyes wander over the array of lotions lined up on Guy's side of the sinks. Belle waited for her to comment on the excess of jars, but instead Lea was all business.

"Let's get you showered."

The double shower unit had been set-up with a shower chair and stool so Belle could use the sliding hand shower while sitting on the chair and leave her towel and clothes on the stool.

Once seated, Belle waited for Lea to give her privacy, but the carer seemed reluctant to leave. "Are you sure you don't want me to help you undress?" Lea jutted her hip, pinning the glass door open.

"Quite sure." Belle's voice echoed off the tiles. "I've done this on my own countless times." The truth was she'd done it twice and both times it had taken an eternity to get her clothes off. "Just help me get this off." She tapped the Velcro knee cast. "And I'll be fine."

* * *

Despite the effort of getting undressed, Belle held the shower head to her neck and felt some of the tension slip away. Washing was a difficult task, but the hot water on her skin worked like balm on blistered lips, soothing the aches and relaxing sore muscles and skin.

Taking care to avoid her eye-patch, she dowsed her hair and let out a long sigh. Maybe it was time to let go of her anger towards Guy. After all, she'd insisted he go. Could she blame him for following his dream? Leaning back, she shampooed her hair and closed her eyes. He probably had an early call on the set and couldn't get to his phone.

She rinsed the shampoo away and let the water wash over her body one last time. Eyes still closed, she imagined what it would be like to be in the water again; the cold shock of hitting the surface and then the caress of the liquid on her skin.

"I see you're managing okay." Lea's voice smashed through the tranquil moment like a hammer.

Belle dropped the shower head and the brushed-steel fitting clanged against the tiles. Shocked and naked, she grappled for the stool and grabbed the towel. "What are you doing in here?" She was shrieking and trying to cover herself at the same time. Water was spraying up and soaking the towel. "I told you to wait outside."

She heard the shower door open, but without her glasses everything was a blur. Lea's arm brushed Belle's shoulder and the sound of rushing water cut out, plunging the bathroom into silence. A silence that was only marred by the sound of Belle's heavy breathing and the last few drips from the shower.

"Here." Another towel was shoved into Belle's hands. She grabbed the dry cloth and held it to her chest. "You didn't tell me to wait outside." Lea's voice was loud in the tiled cubicle. "You said," she spoke slowly, enunciating each word, "just get me in the shower and I'll do the rest. I didn't know I wasn't supposed to check on you."

Shivering now, Belle saw no point in arguing. All she wanted was to dry herself and get dressed. "Okay." She leaned forward, groping for her glasses. "Fine, just go and let me get my clothes on."

"Here." Lea slapped the spectacles into Belle's outstretched hand. "Call me when you're ready."

With water streaming into her good eye and dampening her patch, she fumbled on the glasses in time to see Lea exiting the bathroom. Alone, Belle dropped her head into her hands. The situation with Lea was becoming intolerable. The sooner she spoke to Guy the better.

When Belle emerged from the bedroom, she could hear the caregiver clattering around in the kitchen. Trying to be as quiet as possible, she pushed forward and closed the bedroom door. Still reeling with embarrassment and shock from the incident in the bathroom, she pulled out her phone and called Guy.

"Hi, babe." Guy's voice, so deep and familiar, made her throat tighten with emotion.

"Hi." Now that she had him on the line, she wasn't sure what she wanted to say. *I want to know why you haven't called.* Instead, she made small talk. "How was your flight?"

"Not bad. I got in so late I just crashed. Then they wanted me on set early." She could hear voices in the background and something that sounded like a giant fan whirring. "I wanted to call, but I couldn't get to my phone."

"You don't have to explain, I understand." But did she? He was obviously holding his phone when she called. Why had he waited for her to contact him? "I just wanted to check in and tell you…" Belle wasn't sure how to continue. "Tell you I'm okay."

"That's great, babe. I've been thinking about you. When I get back we should–" There was a burst of sound and his words were muffled.

"What? Guy, what did you say?"

"Sorry, they're calling me." He sounded distracted, impatient to get back to work. "Look, I'll call you tonight."

"Wait." She could hear the desperation in her voice and lowered her tone. "Before you go, can you text me the number for the nursing agency?"

There was a moment's delay before he answered. A second filled with noise and activity in the background. "Why? Is something wrong?" She could imagine him closing his eyes in frustration, wanting to concentrate on the most important job of his career, not her petty gripes with the carer.

"No." She forced a laugh. "Everything's fine. I just wanted to ask them about…" Her mind reached for a plausible reason to ring the agency. "Ongoing part-time help. You know, for when I'm almost recovered."

"Oh, yeah." She could hear the relief in his voice. "Good idea. I'll text you the number as soon as I get a minute. Gotta go. Love you."

Before she could respond, he was gone.

Chapter Seven

Arthur used an old tin mug to scoop birdseed out of the sack. He could hear the birds shrilling, their cries unmistakable and familiar to his attuned ears. They wanted feeding. He grunted, twisted the sack closed and secured it with a rubber band, then dumped the seed in a square container that once housed vanilla ice-cream. Stooping, he balanced the ice-cream tub under one arm and picked up the watering can. One of the things he liked about birds was how uncomplicated they were. Simple creatures wanting nothing more than food and water. Well, he supposed that was the thing about being able to fly, it made everything else seem unimportant.

The aviary had seen better days. Much better days. With its peeling paint and lop-sided roof, it was almost a small replica of the house, both dwellings in the winter of their existence. But Tippi, Rod and Belle didn't care about fancy cages any more than Arthur gave a toss about the old house.

His long raincoat flapped in the morning breeze, and a tuft of hair, like a whitish-brown horn, stood up on his crown as he shuffled across the yard and opened the aviary door.

"Here you go, sweetie." He smacked his lips together, producing a kissing sound, and tipped the seeds into the twin feeder. Tippi was the first to flutter over his shoulder and land on the pile of birdfeed in a flurry of green and red. "Now, you slow down and let the little one have her share."

He glanced over at Belle, still small, her colours not as bright as her parents, but the little bird had watchful eyes. Soulful eyes. Arthur pulled a slender section of branch from the inside pocket of his raincoat.

"Here you go, my darling." He placed the fig tree branch on the perch outside the roost. "Smells nice, huh?" Belle responded by opening her little beak and trilling. Arthur smiled. "I haven't forgotten your water. And..." Arthur turned his head, nodding at Rod, the ever watchful protector. "I've got something for you too." He produced a mandarin from his other pocket and held it up for the male bird to eye.

With the water tub filled, Arthur took a moment to breathe in the calming scent of chalk and honey. His birds had a distinctively sweet aroma. Rainbow lorikeets were considered pests, but no one could deny their splendour. And, as far as Arthur was concerned, they were pleasant company. Before leaving he stole one more glance at the chick. Little Belle was growing into a real beauty.

"Enjoy your breakfast, little one." He knew he sounded like an old fool, but so what. The hatching of the chick was the highlight of his year and watching her grow was a reason to get up in the mornings.

With his birds taken care of, Arthur stowed the watering can and ice-cream tub back in the shed. He had things to do, but first a little nip of whiskey. Shivering and pulling his coat closed, he shuffled back to the house. *Maybe two nips to keep out the cold.*

An hour later and somewhat unsteady on his feet, he stood watching Belle's house. As much as he tried and promised himself he'd keep his distance, he couldn't get her off his mind. She tugged at him like a magnet. He should have learned his lesson last time. And what a lesson that was. Sacked from his post at the university, forced to scurry from the English building in shame. Just thinking about the way his colleagues watched him with accusing eyes made his vein-threaded cheeks burn with shame. Shame and anger.

From his perspective on the driveway, it seemed nothing was going on, but he knew better. The two women were alone. He'd kept a close eye on the place since yesterday and, except for the girl, no one had gone in or out. But staring at the building wasn't enough. He had to get closer to really see the two of them.

He turned and ducked into the trees. The morning light made navigating the property easier, but increased his risk of being seen. Doing his best to hurry from tree to tree, he edged through the bush and moved towards the back of the property.

When he neared the fringe of the trees, he slowed and strained to see the deck. A few metres and he had a view of the back of the house, including the pool, deck, and lawn. He made himself comfortable, sitting at the base of a large silver gum. For now he'd only watch. But soon he'd move closer.

* * *

Belle found Lea in the kitchen making tea. With her back turned and her long dark ponytail swinging, she looked younger. But then Belle didn't know the girl's age. In fact, Belle realised she knew nothing about the caregiver who was sharing her house. Nothing except she had a prosthetic foot. It was a strange and somehow deeply personal thing to know about someone who was almost a stranger.

"I'm making some tea." Lea spoke without turning around. Belle guessed she'd heard the chair approaching. "I thought we could have it on the deck." She turned away from the cups and opened the fridge. "You know, get some fresh air."

At the mention of fresh air Belle realised she really did want to get out of the house. "That sounds nice."

After some manoeuvring and a few false starts, Lea wheeled Belle through the back door and across the deck. The sun was shining, the clear winter sky managing to look flawlessly blue and austere at the same time. Belle took a deep breath, enjoying the smell of damp grass mingled with the sharp odour of chlorine coming off the pool. When Lea went back inside to fetch the cups, Belle wheeled herself closer to the wooden railings so she could stare down on the pool.

The water rippled under a slight breeze. She imagined how shocking it would be to plunge in and felt her heart flutter with excitement. *It won't be long*, she told herself. One of the things that kept her going was the thought of swimming again. *There's air in my lungs, enough to make it to the end of the pool.* Her mantra, the one she used when swimming to push that little bit longer, to go that bit further; it worked it's magic and she felt her thoughts even out. She would swim again, even if she couldn't write she'd still have the water.

"Where do you want it?" Belle turned to see Lea holding two mugs, the steam snaking upwards from the cups and disappearing on the breeze.

"Just here." Belle tapped the flat-top of the railing. "I like looking at the pool."

Lea set the cup down and leaned her hip against the balustrade. "Why did you get such a big pool?"

Belle rubbed her temple, feeling the damp crinkled tape that held the patch in place. The dressing would need to be changed, but she'd do it herself, later. After speaking to Guy, she'd taken her pills and the almost out-of-body feeling that came with the first wave of relief hit her.

"I always wanted to be a swimmer. An Olympic swimmer." She chuckled despite the sudden wave of sadness that threatened to bring tears. "I still like to swim laps." Belle picked up the mug, relishing the warmth in her hands. "At least I used to before the accident."

"Why didn't you?" Lea watched her over the top of her mug, steam making the girl's eyes appear misty. "I mean, why didn't you become a swimmer?"

Belle took a sip of tea before answering. It was hot and sweet. She almost told the girl she didn't take sugar, but decided to bite back the criticism and just enjoy the sunshine. "I was pretty good. Well, there was potential, but..." She tipped her head back and closed her eyes, enjoying the sun on her eyelid. "I was too short. Didn't have the reach to be competitive so I concentrated my efforts on writing." *Now I can't even do that.*

"Did that make up for it?" Lea was staring at the lawn, her elbows on the railing top.

Belle frowned. "What do you mean?"

"Becoming a famous writer, did it make up for not being able to do the thing you loved?"

Belle opened her mouth to answer, but hesitated. *Did it?* She wasn't sure she had an answer. Even if she had been tall enough and pursued her dream, she was thirty-nine. Her competitive days would have been long over. Maybe she could have done both, but she doubted it would have been possible to split herself two ways. No, swimming would have been her life.

"I don't know. Probably not." She had no idea why she was telling Lea something she'd never even shared with Guy. "I'm not complaining. Writing has given me an amazing lifestyle and," she drew out the word. "I do love it."

"But it's not your first choice?" Lea was looking at her now, not just in a casual way, but really staring as though trying to see inside her.

The intensity in the girl's stare made Belle uncomfortable so she deflected the question. "What about you? Did you always want to be a carer?"

Lea looked away, her head turned towards the trees. "No. I was a dancer before."

Belle looked down at Lea's shoes, taking in the way she leaned to the left. Belle knew the pain of being forced to let go of your dreams, but nothing she'd been through compared to what Lea must have experienced. Not letting go, but having it torn away. Suddenly the girl's curt manner and closed off countenance made more sense.

"I'm sorry." Belle watched the back of Lea's head, not knowing if she was upsetting her. "How did it… How did you lose—"

"There's a man hiding in the trees." Lea's voice was calm, unhurried. For a moment Belle wasn't sure she'd heard her correctly. "He's watching us."

The last part hit home and Belle leaned forward too suddenly, knocking the mug off the railing. "Jesus. Are you sure?" Ignoring the mug, she tried to see around the girl and follow her gaze. "Where is he?" Belle's hand crept up to her throat, her fingers circling her neck.

She caught a glimpse of someone on the far right of the lawn. What looked like a shoulder edged out from behind a gum tree. Under her fingers she could feel the blood pulsing in her neck.

"Stay here." Lea pushed off the railing. "I'm going to see what he's up to."

"No." Belle's voice was like the crack of a whip, bouncing off the pool and filling the garden. "You're not confronting some creep hiding in the bushes." Belle's eyes danced between Lea's face and the trees. The shoulder disappeared.

"I'll be okay." A wisp of steamy breath escaped Lea's mouth. She turned to go, but Belle grabbed her wrist.

"No. It's dangerous." Lea's face changed when Belle touched her, the colour in her cheeks leaching away, suggesting shock was setting in. "Let's go inside."

Lea shook off Belle's hand. For a second she thought the girl would bolt for the stairs, but she nodded. The chair bumped over the doorstep, entering with more ease than when they'd exited.

"Lock the door." Belle wasn't sure why she was whispering. "I'll check the patio doors." She pushed through the kitchen, not waiting for Lea to answer.

Belle's fingers were quivering as she tried the lock. Her mind spun trying to remember if there was any other entry point. *He could smash his way in.* The windows were locked, but if he really intended to enter all he had to do was smash a window.

Belle was gnawing at her nails, this time migrating from the thumb to the index finger. The logical thing to do would be to phone the police. A sharp crack split the air making her jump in the chair and jolt her knee. Her head whipped around, tracking the noise. Lea appeared in the dining room, her mouth slightly open as though about to ask a question.

The sound came again and this time Belle's mind worked past shock and panic and recognised it as a knock on the door. A firm no-nonsense knock that demanded immediate attention.

"Shit." Belle looked up into Lea's face. To her surprise, the girl looked composed. "Now what?"

Lea put a finger to her lips and turned back to the kitchen. "Where are you going?" Belle leaned forward in her chair, her voice a whisper. "Lea?"

There was a third knock, this one loud enough to shake the heavy door on its hinges. Belle reached for her phone and remembered she had left it on the bedside table after talking to Guy.

Lea returned with one hand held behind her back. Belle opened her mouth to speak, but the caregiver held up her hand and walked towards the door.

"Are you crazy?" Belle's voice was louder than she intended, but her heart was pounding so violently it was hard to hear herself.

Lea headed into the sitting room. As she approached the front door, Belle could see what she had behind her back. A large can was gripped in her fist. Belle's fleeting reaction was to wonder why the girl chose pineapples. But as the reality of the situation hit home, she let out a cry of alarm and wheeled forward.

"Don't go near the door." Belle's voice was louder now, high and tight with panic. "Lea, don't."

But there was no stopping the carer. Her hand was on the door, turning the knob. Belle thought of heading for the bedroom, grabbing her phone and calling the police, but she couldn't leave Lea alone to face whoever was on the other side of the door. Instead, Belle rolled to a stop halfway into the sitting room and tried to keep her laboured breathing under control.

The door opened inward. Lea stepped to the right, filling the crack so all Belle could see was her back. For a single beat, there was silence.

Chapter Eight

"Where's Belle?" She recognised the croaky voice immediately: Arthur. And, judging by the slushiness of his words, he was drunk.

"She doesn't want to see you." Lea's hand gripping the can moved down almost to her side. "We know you were watching us. Get lost or I'll call the cops." There was steel in the girl's voice, a hard threatening edge than sent a tremor down Belle's spine.

"You'd better get out of my way." Arthur was shouting now, with all the indignation of an angry drunk. "She needs to know what y–"

Lea struck with unexpected suddenness. Arthur was shouting and then there was a thud like the sound a mallet makes hitting a piece of beef. The girl stumbled back and Arthur slumped into the room. A gash hanging open on his forehead.

Belle rammed her fist into her mouth and muffled a scream. His eyes found her and his mouth moved as a line of blood ran into his left eye. Arthur's legs bent, but he managed another step before crumpling to the floor.

Belle was crying now, her shoulders shaking with each sob. "Is he... Did you kill him?" The question seemed absurd, something she couldn't imagine herself having to ask.

Lea set the can on the table near the door. It sat beside a carved bowl that Belle and Guy tossed their keys and loose change into. The girl stood over Arthur, knees slightly bent, head turned in a listening posture.

"No. He's breathing." Her voice was flat, without any trace of fear. "Go in the kitchen and get the extension cord from the back of the fridge. We need to tie him up."

Belle couldn't believe what she was hearing. "No. No, I'm calling the police." The tears had stopped, but her voice still shook. "And an ambulance."

Lea turned from Arthur, her eyes wide with shock or anger, Belle couldn't tell which. "Okay, but it'll take a while for them to get out here. What if he gets up? You heard him. He wanted to get to you." She nudged his leg with her foot.

"Don't." Belle snapped out the word. "Don't touch him."

Lea pointed to Arthur's head. His eyes were closed. "Do you want him coming after you?"

Belle was biting her nails again, wrestling with the idea of tying up an injured man. He'd seemed terrifying when he was shouting for her at the door, but now he looked frail and pathetic.

"Go before he wakes up." Lea stepped behind Belle's chair and turned her around, shoving her towards the kitchen. "I'll watch him."

When Belle returned with the cord, she meant to ask how the girl knew there was an extension cord at the back of the fridge, but the question slipped her mind when she saw Lea crouched beside Arthur. "Look." She turned and held up a knife. "I found this in his jacket." As the girl's wrist moved, a shaft of light bounced off the long blade. "It's a good thing I stopped him before he had the chance to use it."

"Oh, God." Belle grimaced and watched as Lea set the knife down on the rug. She'd always thought there was something strange about the man. Always felt uneasy around him, but never for a moment did she think he was capable of... She pulled her gaze away from the knife. She had no idea what Arthur meant to do with the weapon and, thanks to Lea's quick actions, she would never find out.

Lea was binding the man's hands. He was still out or at least he seemed to be. His arms were limp and heavy looking in Lea's grasp. She tied them in front of him then she sat back on the rug.

"We'll need something for his legs too. Tying his hands is no good if he can get up and run at us." Lea looked around the room. "That will do." She stood, the manoeuvre slightly off balance. Despite the terror of the situation, Belle couldn't help marvelling at how well the girl managed on her prosthetic.

Lea pulled the extension cord out from behind the television and unplugged it. Belle turned back to Arthur and noticed something sticking out of his mouth. She moved in closer then pulled back in surprise.

"Why'd you put your scarf in his mouth?"

Lea was on the move again, bending over Arthur then sitting on the floor next to his feet. "It's better if he can't speak." She had her back to Belle, wrapping the man's ankles with the black extension cord.

Belle lifted her glasses and wiped the bridge of her nose. She had a sinking feeling in her stomach, like things were spiralling out of control. They should be calling the police, not hog-tying the man.

"But he might choke. He might need to–"

"For fuck sake." The anger in Lea's words took her by surprise. "I don't want him yelling and making threats. Do you?"

When she answered, Belle tried to keep her tone even. "This has gone far enough. I'm calling the police."

"I'll do it." Lea scrambled to her feet. "I left my phone upstairs, where's yours?" She held her hand out, waiting for Belle to hand over her phone.

"I left it in the bedroom. I'll go and make the call." Belle pulled back and started turning the chair.

"No." Lea grabbed the handles and pulled her back. "You watch him. It'll be quicker if I go." Before Belle could argue, Lea was out of the room.

The wound on Arthur's head was seeping, the stream of blood had slowed to an ooze that pooled on the rug, forming a dark halo around the man's skull. Belle watched Arthur's unmoving form. He'd come to the house with a purpose, it was clear in his voice when he demanded to see her. And the knife proved his intent. Yet slumped on the floor, head bleeding, he looked older, less like a threat and more like someone who needed help.

Belle moved, turning the chair around, then headed into the kitchen and returned with a clean tea towel. When she returned to the sitting area, she slowed her progress and approached Arthur with caution. He was tied up, but he was still capable of lashing out.

She pulled up near his head. Keeping the chair's wheels out of the blood meant she had to lean low and stretch to place the folded wad of fabric on his wound. When the compress touched his head, Arthur groaned and his eyelids fluttered.

She wanted to say something, tell him she was trying to help him, but he'd come to the house with a knife. He'd been worked up about seeing her. Maybe her voice would only provoke more violence. Instead, Belle held the tea towel to his injured head, hoping applying pressure was the correct course of action.

"What are you doing?" Lea spoke from over Belle's shoulder. For someone with a prosthetic foot, the girl managed to move with stealth.

"I'm trying to stem the bleeding. You'd know more about this sort of thing than me. Is that what I should be

55

doing? I know that's what you're supposed to do with cuts and things, but on the head..." Belle glanced over her shoulder. "Is pressure the right thing?" She was babbling, waiting for Lea to jump in and take over the first aid.

"Mm. Yes, pressure's good. But you shouldn't be touching him. He's dangerous."

The bleeding seemed to be slowing. Belle left the wad of towelling on Arthur's head and sat back. "What did the police say?" She had to turn the chair to look at the girl.

Lea took a long breath and scratched her neck. "The operator said there's a big bushfire just outside of Mandurah so it could be some time before they're able to get an ambulance here."

Lea was moving again, this time towards the kitchen. Belle wanted to follow her and ask for details, but didn't want to leave Arthur alone. Her concern for the man was mostly based on fear. Fear he'd die, but also a stronger more urgent dread that churned in her gut. Belle didn't want to take her eye off the man in case he tore off his bindings and crept up behind her.

"Lea, wait," she called after the carer but got no response. Arthur's legs moved like he was asleep and changing positions.

Belle pulled back and positioned herself at his feet, leaving a metre between the chair's wheels and the unconscious man. The tingle of relief she'd felt after taking her tablets had abated, leaving her nerves raw and her leg aching. It was less than twenty-four hours since her husband left and in that time the world had shifted into a surreal drama that seemed to have no end time.

Lea returned from the kitchen carrying more drinks. Belle wondered if the caregiver knew how to do anything but make endless cups of tea. Belle's mind flashed back to the moment Lea struck Arthur with the can. *She knows how to hurt.* The thought set off a rash of gooseflesh on her forearms.

"I've made coffee." Lea set the cups down on the coffee table. "I think we both need it."

Belle wheeled around the couch. She was wrong about the tea. It seemed Lea's skills also stretched to coffee. She watched the carer lean back into the couch eager to sip from her cup. She looked calm, oblivious to the man tied up on the floor that might or might not be dying.

"How long did the operator say it would take before someone gets here?" Belle's hand crept to her mouth, teeth and fingernails drawn together by anxiety. She forced her hand back into her lap.

Lea shrugged still holding the cup. "An hour and a half, maybe longer."

There was a detached look on the girl's face that reminded Belle of the way doctors looked when they gave you bad news. She had the urge to hit the cup out of Lea's hand, but reminded herself that the carer had most likely saved both of them from being attacked.

"So we just drink coffee and wait?" She couldn't keep the incredulity out of her voice. "What if he dies?"

Lea smiled. It was the first time since she had arrived that Belle had seen the girl's face so animated. "Better him than us."

Chapter Nine

His actions were stiff, his voice an octave too high. The director was whispering to his assistant, his face the colour of an over-ripe plum. Guy was struggling. Everyone on the set could see it. Even his co-star couldn't look him in the eye. Instead, she kept her head buried in a copy of the script, pretending to be going over her lines.

As much as he tried to get into his character, every movement felt forced, every facial expression stretched and amateurish. He'd been waiting his entire adult life for this moment and because of some stupid girl, he was blowing it. No matter how hard he tried, all he could focus on was the text message he'd received just before speaking to Belle:

Your wife's the one who's going to suffer and it will be your fault.

Katrina wasn't going away. He'd been an idiot to think he could just ignore the problem. That's what the girl was: a problem. *No*, he corrected himself, *she's a fucking nightmare.* And, while he was messing up every word in an important scene, Katrina was getting ready to shoot a flaming arrow into his marriage.

Guy snatched up a bottle of water from the catering table. He wasn't really thirsty, but standing around made him nervous. He needed to be doing something with his hands. He tossed the bottle from one hand to the other, trying to watch the director out of the corner of his eye. The conversation between him and his assistant, Andy, was winding up. Andy nodded then headed in Guy's direction.

"Okay. Lunch." The director's voice was booming but with no trace of good humour.

"Are you okay, buddy?" Andy clapped him on the shoulder almost knocking the bottle out of Guy's hand.

Guy looked down into the assistant director's face and noticed his eyes were darting around the set and appeared to be looking for a safe place to land. Andy was a good guy. He'd pushed Guy's name, convincing the director and the studio to take a chance on an almost unknown Aussie actor over other more bankable names. Now Guy was letting him down. Worse than letting him down, he was making him look bad in front of Abraham Lions, a big name director the studio had begged to take on the mid-level action movie that was supposed to be Guy's big break.

"I'm just a bit distracted." Guy twisted the cap on the bottle of water. The headache he'd woken up to thanks to his mini bar spree was ratcheting up into a blinding pain at the back of his eyes. "My wife's still recovering from a car accident and she's at home with a nurse." He could see Andy was only half listening; instead, his attention was on the director's back as the man walked towards his office.

Andy nodded. "Oh, yeah. Yeah, that's tough. But," Andy turned his attention on Guy, "Abraham really wants to get this scene right and..." His eyes narrowed into squints. "...he feels like you don't have the experience to pull it off."

Guy's mouth dropped open and he stepped back. "Christ, Andy. I'm having one bad morning and he's already saying I'm not good enough."

Andy made a flapping motion with his hands, signalling Guy to calm down. "I know. I know, but it's the *first* morning." He took a step closer and lowered his voice. "His last movie tanked and he's got a lot invested in this picture. You just need to relax and show him what you can do."

"I'm trying. But I told you, my wife's–"

Andy's face changed from sympathetic to stony. "We've all got stuff going on. You need to put that shit out of your mind and focus."

Guy could feel his throat tightening. His big opportunity was slipping away. Everything he'd fought for was turning to shit and he was whining like a baby. Suddenly his costume felt heavy as though lined with lead. He wanted to tear off the artfully cuffed leather jacket and torn shirt so his skin could breathe.

"I will." He was having trouble getting the words out. "It's just nerves. I'll be okay after lunch." He forced his face into an expression he hoped looked confident while on the inside his heart was in his throat.

Andy's expression softened. "I know you will." He gave Guy another clap on the back. "I'm going to send Warren to your dressing room in about fifteen minutes." Guy had seen Warren on the set of his last movie. He was a sort of scene guru. He knew how to get the best out of people but didn't have the looks or charisma to be an actor. Instead of being in front of the camera, he helped actors prepare for emotional scenes, nude scenes, and all the stuff that made them nervous. Or, in Guy's case, pull him back from turning a simple scene into a train wreck.

"Thanks, mate." Guy swallowed and looked down at his hands. "I really appreciate everything you're doing for me."

When Andy spoke, his voice was friendly and relaxed again. "No problem, buddy. I know you'll do a great job." Despite the encouragement, they both knew this was Andy's way of giving Guy one last chance before the director contacted the studio and asked to have him replaced.

In his dressing room, Guy peeled off the jacket and draped it over the costume stand. The shirt he wore looked lightweight, but was in fact made of some sort of coarse material that clung to his skin like a rash. The buttons were fake; the only way to remove it was by pulling it over his head, but with heavy make-up coating his face he couldn't risk staining the white fabric.

Trying to ignore the way his skin burned, he stared at the dressing table in the corner. Not wanting to have to look at it, he'd put his phone in the drawer. But out of sight out of mind hadn't worked so far. And, after Katrina's last message, he had to know if she'd contacted his wife.

Guy pulled open the drawer and snatched up the phone. To his relief there were no new messages. But that didn't mean Katrina hadn't contacted Belle. For all he knew she was speaking to her right now. His head was aching, the pain buzzing in his ears like static. Katrina had said Belle would be the one to suffer. It hadn't occurred to him before that she meant anything but emotional suffering. But now, thousands of kilometres from home, Guy wondered if the girl was capable of more than threats and nasty text messages.

Not really sure where his thoughts were going, he called his wife. When the call went straight to voicemail, Guy spat out a stream of curses and kicked the dresser, sending it clattering against the wall. The dressing rooms were small wooden cubicles, hastily knocked together structures that offered little in the way of privacy. He had to get his emotions under control before every person on the set was talking about him.

Breathing heavily from the minor exertion, he closed his eyes and held the phone to his forehead, willing himself to think, to be calm. Warren would be knocking on his door in a few minutes. He had to act now or he wouldn't get another chance for hours.

Arthur. Guy's shoulders relaxed. Belle didn't like their neighbour, but Guy suspected that was more about her own hang-ups than anything the man had done. Besides, there was no one else even close that he could ask to check on his wife.

Guy called Arthur, but just like Belle's phone it went straight to voicemail. "Shit." He spat out the word and tossed the mobile on the dressing table.

He ran his fingers through his hair and they came away stained. The hair and make-up crew had dyed his hair before shooting started, turning his blonde to black in twenty minutes. He caught sight of himself in the mirror over the dressing table and blinked back his surprise. With his teeth gritted and the dark hair, he hardly recognised himself.

He'd never planned on cheating. And for the first year he hadn't looked at another woman, but then everything changed. A wrap on the door halted his thoughts. Without waiting for him to answer, Warren pulled open the thin wooden door.

"We're wrapping up." Warren's round face was pale and there was a thin sheen of sweat covering his skin.

"What? Why?" Guy tried to stop himself but he had to know. "Is it because of me?"

Warren shook his head. "No." His voice was flat, impatient. "Why do actors think everything is about them?"

Guy let the man's insult roll over him. "Then why?"

"Abraham's had a heart attack. They're waiting for the paramedics." He raised his plump shoulders and his neck disappeared. "That's it. Everyone goes home."

Guy felt the air go out of his lungs and suddenly the room was too small. "For how long?"

Warren didn't answer straight away. His brown eyes narrowed. "He's conscious or at least he was five minutes ago. Thanks for asking."

Guy opened his mouth to defend himself, but Warren cut him off. "Go back to the hotel. Andy will call you later."

Chapter Ten

Listening to the oldies station seemed fitting when driving a vintage Holden. Belle was having a good day. Maybe the best day she'd experienced since she'd quit drinking. The craving was still there, sitting at the edge of her thoughts like a waiting tiger. But today the tiger was drowsy and Belle's mind was free to enjoy the drive.

She tossed a strand of blonde hair over her shoulder and turned onto the side road that led to the bridge. When Guy called from Sydney, he was upbeat, almost dizzy with excitement. His audition had gone well and he thought he stood a good chance at the part of a lifetime. *Now if he just gets the job, I can stop worrying.*

The last time she'd managed to write something was over a year ago. She had money, the last book was still selling, and the movie rights were a major boost to her bank balance, but it wouldn't last forever. Not the way Guy liked to spend. She thought of his thirty-two pairs of designer sunglasses and his sleek sports car and her fingers clenched on the steering wheel. He wanted a lifestyle she could no longer provide, not if she couldn't get past the worst case of writer's block she'd ever experienced.

She'd promised herself she wouldn't worry about money, not when things were going well for her husband, and she was happily, if not productively, sober. Yet even as she rolled back her shoulders and tried to enjoy the beauty of the autumn morning, a flat cynical voice whispered in her ear. If she couldn't give Guy the lifestyle he craved, he'd find it elsewhere. *No.* She pulled herself back from the destructive thoughts. Her husband loved her and she loved him. Whatever happened, they'd work it out.

The streets were almost deserted. The only other vehicle she'd seen was an old four-wheel drive, but as they passed a side street, even that disappeared. With the windows down, the sharp salty tang in the air told her she was nearing the ocean. She loved her swimming pool, but the sea was calling. She planned on swimming for a good half an hour before lazing on the beach in a little spot she loved just past Falcon.

The road stretched out like a dark carpet, cutting through the tangle of trees as sun dappled the windscreen. Belle tapped her fingers on the wheel, keeping up the beat while singing along with a 1950s crooner. She rolled through a deserted intersection and let rip with the chorus.

"You took the part that once was my heart so why not take all of—"

An explosion rocked the car and Belle's face whacked the side window in a thunderous rain of glass and steel and screaming rubber...

Belle gulped in a breath and her head jerked up. Her eyelids were sticky, like they were glued shut. She'd had countless dreams about the accident, but never one so vivid. Still panting and with the sound of bone snapping still in her ears, she rubbed her palms into the corners or her eyes and managed to get them open. Her surroundings were a haze of shadowy colour, but she could feel the softness of the sofa beneath her. The last thing that came to mind was letting Lea help her onto the sofa so she could drink her coffee; after that, the edges of her recollection were frayed.

Reaching out, she patted her hand on the cushions, searching for her glasses. Had she taken them off? Being without her spectacles or contacts always left her feeling just short of panicked. Her fingers found the plastic frames wedged into the back of the sofa.

With her glasses on, she could see how late it was. Gloomy light tinged purple by the setting sun stalked through the blinds. She sat up and reached for her phone, only remembering she had left it in the bedroom when her hand landed on her empty pocket. *That's not right. I didn't leave it. Lea took it.*

Everything came rushing back: the man hiding in the trees, Arthur pounding on the door, and Lea hitting him with a tin of pineapples. Belle swivelled her head around, searching for the caregiver. Was it possible the police had come and gone while she slept? Almost as soon as the idea popped into her mind she dismissed it as ridiculous. The front door was less than eight metres away from the sofa. There was no way police or paramedics could have come into the house without waking her.

Belle was about to call out when a sound came from the other side of the sofa; a huff of air, like a dog snuffling the dirt. She stopped moving and listened, and again heard a grunt then shuffling.

"Lea," Belle called, her voice cracking on the last vowel. She forced herself to wait, counting to five before calling out again.

Belle reached three when the snuffling turned into a muffled cry. "Lea?" She put more force into the word this time.

Belle's back was to the archway, making her have to twist at the waist and angle her head to see if the girl was coming. The area leading to the kitchen sat in shadows. Apart from the sounds coming from the other side of the sofa there was only silence. It was then that it occurred to her that Arthur might have done something to Lea.

Half pushing with her good leg and at the same time using her arms to gain purchase on the top of the sofa, Belle looked over the cushion. Arthur still lay bound, but now on his back and staring up at her. When their eyes met Belle felt a spike of panic and sank again into the sofa.

If he'd managed to break free, why would he be on his back draped in cord and wearing the gag? If Arthur was still bound, where was Lea? *Where are the police?*

Belle scanned the room and spotted her wheelchair parked near the window. She couldn't just sit and wait, not with Arthur bound and gagged a few metres away. Besides, she needed to pee.

"Shit." She mumbled out the word and edged her legs over the side of the sofa.

With no sign of Lea, Belle would have to reach the chair on her own steam. The surgery to repair her torn ligaments and tendons was healing nicely, at least in the surgeon's opinion, but her snapped patella was still wired together and would remain so for another month. The three metres to her chair would be the furthest she'd gone alone since the accident. Just the thought of putting weight on her knee set off a shiver of anticipatory pain.

Before standing she called Lea one more time, but the girl didn't answer. Still mumbling a string of curses, Belle pushed herself up and balanced on her good leg. Her right leg, weak from lack of use, trembled under the strain.

"I can do it," she told herself. *There's air in my lungs, enough to make it to the end of the pool.*

The first hop was the hardest. When her right foot left the floor, she felt a split second of terror, certain when she landed the leg would give out and send her sprawling onto the rug. But her right leg held, wobbled, but stayed under her.

Balancing on the edge of the sofa, Belle continued to hop, counting as she moved and using the furniture to keep her steady. Behind her, Arthur's grunts and cries grew louder.

Her short hair clung to the nape of her neck in damp wisps. The chair sat only a hop away, but her leg shook as though ready to give out. With nothing between her and the wheelchair, Belle took the final jump and as she landed her right leg bowed. Without thinking she put her injured leg down to stop herself from falling.

The pain was like nothing she'd ever felt, even eclipsing the memory of the accident itself. She shrieked out a tortured sound that echoed in the sitting room, more like the wails of an injured animal than anything human. Unsure how she managed to remain standing, much less moving, she grabbed the chair and hop-shuffled into it as tears dripped down her cheeks.

As an exhausted huff of air left her lungs, she felt a stir of anger. Anger at Guy for leaving her when she needed him, but mostly at Lea. It was her job to be here when she needed her. While it wasn't the girl's fault that Arthur had turned up and tried to get into the house, Belle couldn't help thinking everything had started to go wrong when the carer arrived. And Lea's brand of care was sketchy at best.

Belle dragged her hand across her streaming nose and wheeled towards the bedroom. When she rounded the sofa, she hesitated. Arthur's head twisted in her direction and his jaw worked, as though trying to speak around the gag. She felt a stab of guilt and pulled to a stop.

"I'm sorry, Arthur. I don't like this any more than you do, but…" She pushed her glasses up on her nose, trying to find the words to justify what Lea had done to him. "You were out of control… dangerous." She lowered her voice and leaned forward slightly. "You scared me."

His eyes, brown and watery, moved between Belle's face and the archway. Belle pulled back, not sure if she saw anger or fear in the man's jittery gaze. He rattled off a stream of incoherent words and then let his head drop back on the floor.

"I'm going to call the police again." As she spoke, Belle pushed her wheels towards the archway. "We need to get this sorted out."

There was no sign of Lea in the bedroom. Belle raised herself a few inches out of the chair and snapped on the light. With the long shadows chased away, she headed straight to the bathroom and used the toilet, thankful she'd thought to buy a disabled toilet chair to go over the bowl. It made using the toilet easier, if not effortless.

Back in the bedroom, she grabbed her water bottle from the nightstand and took a long drink, then dropped the bottle in her lap. Her mouth felt papery and coated as though she had slept too heavily. With her knee throbbing, she thought of taking a couple of her painkillers, but her mind was still cloudy from sleep so she settled on two paracetamol.

When she reached the dresser, she noticed an empty space between the paracetamol and anti-inflammatory tablets. The painkillers were gone. Belle gave her head a slight shake and looked around the bedroom. Could Lea have picked them up and put them somewhere else by mistake? But that didn't make sense because the last time she had her pills was in the morning and she'd taken them herself before they went out on the deck.

Belle reached up and put her finger on the empty space where the pills belonged. She was certain she had counted two tablets into her palm then put the bottle back in its spot. Confused, she tried to work her way through the morning's sequence of events, looking for some logical explanation. But her mind kept coming back to the papery feeling in her mouth and the deepness of her nap on the sofa.

Her stomach turned, a heavy rolling like an empty wine bottle in the surf, undulating with sickening slowness. Something was out of whack. *There's a man bound and gagged on my sitting room floor, of course something's out of whack.* But there was more to it than Arthur. And as much as she didn't want to admit it, things had been strange since Lea arrived. And now her pills were missing and she felt like she'd been drugged.

It was time to call the police. If they were cut off from help by a bushfire, Belle wanted to hear it from the operator herself. She popped two paracetamol out of the blister pack and tossed them in her mouth, then swallowed them with another sip from the water bottle.

Her phone should have been on the nightstand. At least that's where she thought Lea would have left it. But the mobile was nowhere in sight. Had the caregiver taken her phone as well as her tablets? Belle raised her hand and gnawed at the ragged edge of her thumbnail. What possible reason could Lea have for taking her things? *Could the girl be an addict?* Belle tasted blood on her tongue and pulled her thumb out of her mouth.

It made sense, sort of. Lea was strange, almost deadpan most of the time. Could the girl be on something? An image of Lea smashing the can into Arthur's head flashed in Belle's mind. Remembering the *thunk* as the tin collided with flesh made Belle shudder. The carer had morphed from calm to violent in a heartbeat. Was it a stretch then that the girl was taking something – drugs, pills, maybe even crack?

Belle needed help. If Lea had her phone, she'd find another way. She wheeled through to the dining room, intending to go to her office, but movement caught her eye. She spun back towards the sitting room and spotted Lea crouched over Arthur. The man's legs were ratcheting up and down like he was trying to push himself out of the girl's reach.

"Lea." At the sound of Belle's voice, the girl's head whipped around, her dark ponytail flying. "What are you doing?" There was accusation in Belle's voice, but she didn't care.

Lea half turned and held up a bottle of water. "I'm giving him a drink." She turned back to Arthur whose legs were still in motion. "What did you think I was doing?"

Belle pushed forward. Rolling across the room, she came to a stop near Arthur's feet. Lea's body obscured the man's head. "Where were you? I was calling you."

Lea rocked back on her heels and stood looking down on Belle. "I was out back." She tucked the water bottle under her arm. "I needed some air. Is that all right with you?" The petulance in the girl's voice took Belle by surprise.

Belle bit back an angry retort. "I was only asking because I was worried." It was partly true. She had been concerned that by some form of magic Arthur had freed himself, hurt the caregiver, and then miraculously re-tied himself.

"Well..." Lea stepped around the wheelchair and flopped down on the sofa. "You can stop worrying, I'm fine. Just needed a minute to myself." She leaned forward, dumped the water bottle on the coffee table, letting it roll on its side, then massaged her right knee.

Belle had the urge to pick the bottle up and set it on its base. Instead, she watched the girl's fingers kneading her leg and couldn't help wonder if she was in pain. *Maybe that's why she took my pills.* She felt a jab of sympathy, all too aware of how excruciating leg trauma could be. But that still didn't make it okay.

"Where's my phone?" Belle tried to keep the urgency out of her voice, but with each passing minute she was becoming more uneasy.

Lea didn't look up. "I don't know. In your bedroom, I suppose." When she spoke, her eyebrows drew down in a sharp V.

Belle snatched a glance at Arthur. His face was wet as though Lea had spilt water over him. The gag was still in his mouth, but he'd stopped trying to speak.

71

"No." Belle spoke slowly, careful to keep her voice calm. "It's not in there. Where did you put it?"

"Jesus, Belle." Lea's head jerked up. Her eyes were wide and glassy like over-polished blue marbles. "I don't know where you leave your stuff."

Belle recoiled from the anger in the girl's voice, noticing she'd dropped the Mrs Hammer and was now calling her Belle.

Chapter Eleven

A jarring bleep dragged Guy from a deep dream-filled sleep. Next to him, a shape moved. He sat up and snatched up his phone, his body and mind going from blurry to heart-pounding in the second it took to reach the mobile. The display told him it was 10:14. Scrubbing a hand over his face, he saw Andy's number and his pulse evened out a fraction.

"Guy." Andy's voice was husky like he'd been talking for hours. "Did I wake you?" Before Guy could respond, Andy was talking again. "Abraham's out of the woods, but the doctor wants him resting for at least two weeks, so we're sending everyone home."

Sitting naked in the darkened hotel room, Guy felt his body slacken. It was over before it had ever really started. When this sort of thing happened, studios sometimes shelved projects for years.

"We'll let you know when things get back on track. Don't worry about your airfare. The studio's picking up the bill." He could hear Andy talking, but his words were little more than white noise, adding to the ringing in Guy's head.

There was silence on the line and Guy realised it was his turn to speak. "Um." His mind was spinning as he tried to think of something to say. "Which hospital is Abraham in? I'll send flowers or something. Maybe I should visit before I leave."

"Hmm." Now it was Andy's turn to struggle with a response. Guy could almost see the man squirming. "He's not allowed visitors right now, but I'll pass on your regards."

"Okay." The girl in Guy's bed rolled over. He felt her fingers running up his spine. "Thanks for everything you're doing for me, mate. I really appreciate–"

"Sorry, Guy. I've got to go. My other phone's ringing." The call clicked off and the room was silent.

"Shit." Guy dropped his head into his hands and laced his fingers through his now dark hair.

"Everything okay?" Her voice was soft in the darkness. Sandy or Stacey, Guy wasn't sure.

"Yeah. No worries." He spoke without turning around and heard the girl let out a sleepy sigh, then the rustle of sheets as she nestled back into the bed.

He should have told her to go. Hell, he shouldn't have picked her up in the first place, but the idea of being alone was harder to deal with than the endless procession of one-night stands. He was hurting Belle, even if she didn't know about the girls. What he kept doing – the randomness of sleeping with strangers – was gnawing away at their marriage.

He stood and poured himself a drink. No mini bar stuff this time. He'd bought a bottle on the way back to the hotel. He was drinking too much; the signs were clear in his bloodshot eyes. But knowing you're doing something harmful doesn't mean you know how to stop doing it. He, better than anyone, knew doing the wrong thing was an easy choice.

He picked up his glass and crossed the room. He slipped into the bathroom and turned on the light. Like earlier in the day, his reflection startled him. For a moment he couldn't look away. He'd sacrificed everything to get where he was and now it was all fucked up and he didn't know how to put things back together.

He turned away from the mirror and sat on the edge of the tub. The bathroom smelled like puke. Probably Stacey or Sandy. He couldn't remember if her name started with an 'S' or a 'K'. She'd hit the vodka pretty hard when they got back to the room. Guy took a gulp from the glass and grimaced. He'd tried to tell himself it was Katrina's fault, but things were out of control long before he met her.

He was selfish. A selfish prick. He knew that but he'd never actually hurt anyone before. He could live with not being the noblest man in the world, but when he considered what he had done, the pain he'd caused... He shook his head trying to rid his mind of the memory. But no matter how much he drank or lost himself in nameless girls, the guilt clung to him like a stench that couldn't be washed away in a sea of booze and sex.

* * *

Belle glanced at Arthur and noticed his eyes were closed and a thick string of drool hung from the corner of his mouth. It would be dark soon. The thought of spending the night with her neighbour trussed up on the sitting room floor made her scalp prickle with anxiety, not to mention Lea's unpredictable behaviour.

"Can you call my phone?" Belle waited, watching the girl raise her head from where it lolled back on the top of the sofa.

When Lea answered, her voice was sharp – impatient. "What?"

Belle licked her lips. Lea couldn't be more than twenty-five, but in less than twenty-four hours she'd managed to take over the house and, to Belle's shame, intimidate her. "If you ring my phone, we'll be able to track it down."

There was a pleading in Belle's voice that made her want to squirm in her chair. *When did I become so pathetic?*

"My phone's upstairs. I'll do it later." Lea lowered her head. "I need a nap."

Belle wheeled herself closer to the sofa, not sure she'd heard the girl correctly. "You can't be serious?" Belle waved her hand in Arthur's direction. "We can't just leave him there. He's got a head injury. What if–"

Lea lunged with a suddenness that made Belle wince. "What do you want me to do, Belle?" The last word came out dripping with scorn. "Do you want me to drive through a bushfire?" Before Belle could answer, Lea was on her feet and around the sofa. "Do you want me to untie him and give him his knife back?" As she spoke she nudged Arthur with the tip of her shoe. "Because I can do that if you want?"

"No. No. That's not what I meant. I just want my phone." Belle knew by continuing to ask she was making things worse, but they were in her house. Lea was supposed to be helping her. The girl worked for her, so didn't she have the right to ask for her phone? "I need to speak to my husband. He'll be worried."

Lea clamped her hands to the side of her head. "Stop pestering me." She punctuated the last word by drawing her leg back and landing a kick to Arthur's side.

The man let out a muffled cry and raised his head. Belle's mouth dropped open with a jaw-popping creak. For a moment both women were silent. The air in the sitting room seemed too thin, making it difficult for Belle to fill her lungs. Something had shifted. She could see it in the way Lea's blue eyes regarded her. There was a dropping away of control. The caregiver's features seemed to shift into a new countenance, one that was hard and watchful.

When Belle was able to get her mouth working, she chose her next words with care. "I'm sorry." Lea's head tilted to the left like an attentive bird. "I shouldn't have nagged you."

Lea nodded, her chin moving up and down slowly, almost mechanically. She glanced down at Arthur and seemed surprised to find him still lying at her feet. Without speaking she walked around the sofa and sat down. The situation with Lea had gone from unsettling to downright terrifying in the blink of an eye. Even if both of her legs were working, Belle would have been afraid; but half blind and unable to stand on her own two feet, she experienced a feeling of helplessness – a sick dread she hadn't known since childhood.

Maybe it was the sudden violence or perhaps watching someone helpless being victimised that stirred a memory buried so deep that when it surfaced, Belle's mind seemed to fold on itself. She remembered being in a big department store and letting go of her mother's hand. She wasn't supposed to touch things because her mum said she'd break something. But it was nearly Christmas and the aisles were decorated with red baubles and tin soldiers. To Belle the shop seemed like a wonderland and smelled like marshmallows, and she was wearing red sneakers with gold ribbons instead of laces. She liked the way the crinkly soles squeaked when she walked. She wanted so badly to hold the chocolate brown teddy with the big red bow, the one under the Christmas tree with all the lights.

Her mum was talking to a lady in a white top and black pants. She reminded Belle of the dentist and her childish mind wondered if the dentist worked in the department store as well as the clinic where she checked children's teeth. But the thought was fleeting, swallowed up by images of scratch and sniff stickers, and Barbie toothbrushes, and before she knew it, Belle was standing in front of the teddy.

As her slightly sticky fingers reached out to touch its chocolate-coloured fur, a hand fell on her shoulder. "All on your own?" The man spoke in a happy voice and she wondered if he was a friend of her dad's.

Belle let her thumb creep up to her lips and shook her head. The man moved in front of her with his hand still on her shoulder, his big body blocking her view of the teddy.

"You like that teddy?" He smiled and she noticed one of his teeth was brown. Not like the pretty chocolate of the bear, but a nasty brown that reminded her of poop. It occurred to her that the dentist might want to look at the man's tooth. He reached around and grabbed the bear. "Because it's Christmas, I'm going to buy you this bear."

Belle's eyes moved between the man's mouth and the bear. She wasn't supposed to talk to strangers, but a stranger wouldn't be so friendly. A stranger wouldn't want to buy her a teddy.

He reached into his pocket. "Oh, no." He set the bear down and Belle felt tears stinging her eyes. Was he just teasing her about buying the bear? "I left my wallet in the car." His hand slid down her arm. His fingers grabbed her hand.

Belle turned, trying to see her mum, but there were so many people, and the Christmas music was blaring from all corners of the store. The man's hand squeezed hers; his skin felt raspy and hard.

"I can't go outside without asking my mummy." She was trying to make the man understand, but he just nodded and pulled her towards the doors.

One of her ribbon laces came loose and her feet tangled. As the doors whooshed open, Belle tripped and her knee grazed the rough carpet, the stuff with the lines that people were supposed to wipe their shoes on. She started to cry and looked around for her mother, but the man jerked her to her feet and through the sliding doors.

"Stop crying." His voice wasn't friendly anymore. He sounded really cross with her.

She tried to snatch her hand away, but his grip was too strong and when she turned back the shop doors had closed. Her tummy rolled over and for the first time in her short life, Belle experienced real terror. Not the afraid-of-the-dark sort of fear, but something that came from deep in her chest and made her throat close up until she couldn't get her breath. As the sliding doors grew smaller and distant, it was like everything safe and normal had disappeared with them. The parking lot was another world – a world of nightmares.

Belle pushed her glasses up and wiped her eye. "I need some air." The words came out as a series of gasps.

Without waiting for Lea to respond, Belle turned the chair and headed for the kitchen. Her mind was still skidding back and forth between memories she only half knew she possessed and the sound Arthur made when Lea kicked him in the ribs. With each revolution of the wheels she expected the carer's hand to fall on her shoulder, just like… Belle drove the thought away by counting the flicks of her wrists as she pushed the wheels.

Still breathless and with the after-burn of the memory fluttering behind her eyes, Belle stopped. She was at the back door, tears blurring her vision. Whatever she'd remembered, no matter how painful it was, her pressing problem was in the here and now. She had to slow down and focus on getting help. Whatever suppressed memories Lea had awoken didn't matter. *But it does matter. If it's real, it matters a great deal.*

Belle glanced over her shoulder and was relieved to see the caregiver hadn't followed her. She could go out the back door, but then what? Use the ramp and go where? The lawn would be damp. Even if she made it around the side of the house, what then? Push herself all the way down the gravel driveway and onto the road? She doubted she'd make it more than ten metres on the loose stones.

Her hand touched the knob and hung there, fingers lingering on the door. There had to be a better way. She just needed to get her head around it. Lea had her phone and for some reason refused to return it. Belle had no idea why the girl was behaving so erratically. Maybe when Arthur tried to force his way in it had pushed the carer over the edge. But whether or not Arthur was still a risk, Belle couldn't stand by and watch the girl hurt him. And how long would it be before Lea turned on her?

Belle let go of the knob and looked around the kitchen, noticing the breakfast dishes were still on the table. The toasted sandwich maker was open on the counter, a thick layer of burnt cheese clung to the black metal plates. She hadn't noticed this morning but now realised the caregiver had left last night's dishes on the counter. It was a small thing, but a sign that something had been wrong before Arthur showed up.

Still grappling with what to do next, Belle realised she'd been in the kitchen too long. If Lea was listening, she'd be waiting for the back door to open. Belle grabbed the knob and opened the door. She counted to ten guessing that's how long it would take to negotiate her way out the back door. Satisfied she'd waited long enough she closed the door with enough force to rattle the frame.

Now what? Now, Belle decided, she needed to contact someone. The police or Guy or anyone who could send help. But without her phone she was cut off from the outside world. There was no landline in the house, only... Belle's heart skipped a beat. The answer was so obvious she couldn't believe she hadn't thought of it sooner. The modem! She could use the laptop in the study to contact someone.

Moving slowly, sticking to the far wall and trying to cross the dining room as silently as possible, she made her way to the study. Noticing the door was ajar gave her pause. She was the only person who used the room at the far side of the stairs. The door should have been closed. Not wanting to think about Lea creeping around her study, she pushed the door and wheeled inside.

Two large windows spilled more light into the little study than any other room in the house. Looking out over the back lawn and being able to see the natural bush surrounding her house had always inspired her. But now the room was in shadows and the large expanse of sky outside the big windows looked sinister and wild with soot-coloured clouds covering the sinking sun.

Belle didn't need light to find her desk. She'd spent hundreds of hours in this room over the past five years and knew every corner as though it were tattooed on her brain. Although much of the last thirteen months had been spent staring at a blank virtual page, she still liked the privacy of her writing space. The smell of honeysuckle that drifted up from the diffuser on the shelf and the collection of smooth pebbles and scraps of driftwood that filled a basket on her desk; all the things that were familiar and comforting scarcely registered as she crossed the room and flipped open her laptop.

Lea thought she was outside getting fresh air. If Belle took too long, the girl might come looking for her. The last thing she wanted was another confrontation. Belle tapped the keys and the screen lit up. She had no idea if it was possible to contact emergency services online and didn't have time to waste finding out. It would be better, she decided, to contact her sister and then Guy through Facebook. A quick message asking both to contact the police and send help would have to do.

Please let Bethany be checking her Facebook. Belle's lip moved without sound as she brought up the Internet browser. Without realising it, she'd clasped her hands together in a praying pose. Hunched over, intent on the screen, her one eye blinked in disbelief when the page showed an error.

"No. No, not now." Vaguely aware that she was speaking, she pushed the laptop aside and stared at the shiny square on the desk's surface surrounded by a fine ring of dust where the modem usually sat.

Her shoulders dropped and she sat back in the chair. Lea had taken the modem and Ethernet cable just like she'd taken her pills and her phone. Up until now she'd been able to convince herself that the girl was behaving erratically for any number of reasons: she was an addict and wanted the pills *or* what happened with Arthur had sent the carer into shock. Both were plausible reasons, but no longer valid in the face of deliberateness that included systematically cutting Belle off from the rest of the world.

She stared at the screen, no longer seeing the page. Her thoughts now returned to the previous night. Something had nagged at her about Lea's appearance when she returned from checking outside. Belle remembered noticing the girl was wearing trainers. At the time it was just something that she took in without really processing the information. But now Belle realised there were two things wrong with the picture of the girl in trainers and pyjamas. If she'd been awoken by a noise, wouldn't she run downstairs in bare feet? Or even if she did take the time to put on trainers, would she stop to lace them? And they were laced. Belle remembered that quite clearly. The other thing that bothered her was the trainers were dry when Lea came back inside. The back lawn was damp when they were outside this morning. This time of year the grass was always damp at night. If Lea had been outside and, as she'd said, checked the lawn and around the trees, her trainers should have been wet.

Belle's arms were shaking so badly that she let her hands drop into her lap and pressed them together. Lea had been up to something before Arthur appeared on the scene. The realisation was like a smack in the face. Only instead of making her skin sting, it set off a tremble that ran the entire length of her body.

"What are you doing?"

Belle hadn't heard the girl approaching.

Belle slammed the laptop closed. "I was going to write something." She turned the chair so she could see the caregiver and watch her expression. "I've been hashing out ideas for a new story." Her voice was tight so she shrugged her shoulders, trying to relax. "When something comes to me, I have to jot it down or it's gone."

82

Lea's face showed no emotion. "What did you write?"

"What?" Belle had heard the question, but was caught off guard and tried playing for time.

Lea tilted her head to the left and for the second time that day the girl reminded her of a bird. Still watchful, but with a hint of something predatory in the angle of her head and the steadiness of her gaze. "I said what did you write?"

"Nothing." Belle waved a hand in the air. "By the time I got the laptop turned on the thought was gone."

Lea moved quickly, swooping forward with such suddenness that Belle ducked slightly. But to her relief, Lea swept past her and grabbed the handles of the wheelchair. The girl pushed Belle out of the study and gave the chair a shove, sending Belle rolling into the dining room while behind her Lea slammed the study door.

The force of the push sent Belle careening into the dining table. With only a split second to grasp the wheels, she managed to turn the chair and hit the table with her right side. Her good knee smacked the edge of the table leg with enough force to make her gasp with pain. The bump stung, but if it had been her injured knee Belle thought she might have passed out with the pain.

"That was your fault." Lea spoke from behind her and took hold of the chair. "If I didn't have to go running around checking on you, the chair wouldn't have slipped out of my hands."

The push had been deliberate, maybe even in warning, but Belle didn't risk arguing. "Sorry." The word tasted bitter in her mouth.

Lea pushed her back towards the sitting room. "I'm getting worried about you, Belle." The girl raised her voice, making sure Arthur could hear her. "You rush off to the study to write and then can't remember a word of what you had in your mind." Lea made a clicking sound with her tongue. "And I know you've been overdoing it with your painkillers."

"What? No, I haven't." Belle stuttered out the denial and felt a flood of heat on her cheeks.

"That's not true, Belle." Lea rolled the chair past the sofa, but didn't stop. "I saw you taking extra last night." She leaned down, her mouth close to Belle's ear. "It's dangerous and sad when people get addicted to painkillers." The girl's voice was a stage whisper, her breath hot on Belle's ear.

Belle tried to control herself, but couldn't stop her voice rising with outrage. "I'm not addicted to them. I just had a car accident."

"Did you?" Lea's voice dropped, her tone deep and questioning.

Belle snatched a look at Arthur. His head was up and he was watching their movements with watery eyes. He looked as baffled by what was happening as Belle.

"Stop pushing me." Belle turned in the chair, but Lea looked unfazed. "Take your hands off my chair." Belle was shouting now and twisting around, but the chair kept going.

When they reached the bedroom, Belle felt another shove and found herself sailing into the room. Not quick enough to turn this time, the chair struck the bed, but luckily for Belle, the armrest took the impact. By the time she managed to turn around, the door was already closing.

"I think you should cool off in here for a while." Lea was smiling, the sort of sad grin a mother might use on a disobedient child. Before closing the door, the carer paused and the smile was gone. "Don't try to come out or I might lose my cool again." The door closed with a dry clunk.

Chapter Twelve

Joan shrugged into Roger's old wax jacket. For a second she caught a whiff of Larimax Throat Lozenges but the more she tried to capture the smell, the fainter it grew. Just as it was with memories, a comforting scent was like a will-o'-the-wisp; little more than a ghostly essence gone before she could hold it close.

"Don't worry, darling. I'm not getting upset, just sentimental in my old age." She spoke to the empty kitchen. In her mind's eye she could almost see Roger pushing his glasses up so they sat atop his silver hair, a good-natured smile softening his stony features. A smile he kept just for her.

Talking to her husband eased the pain. Not completely, but it helped. Like Roger's smile, it softened the cold edges. Grief was a cruel companion, always at her side silent and ominous. Sometimes the silence in the house was more than she could bear. Most people would think her foolish, prattling on like Roger was still alive *and* listening, but the alternative was too grim. Besides, Joan liked to believe he *was* listening. There were times like last night when she was brushing her teeth, she felt just for a split second that he was next to her. The sensation had been so real that she'd stopped brushing and turned around.

"Best to keep moving." She lifted the collar of the oversized raincoat and tucked her now mostly grey bob inside. "And," she picked up the clear plastic box from the counter, "I've saved us one for later." Her voice dropped to a whisper. "I know you love lamingtons and…" Joan pressed her lips together and dropped her chin.

She had good days and bad days, but some days were grey. Bleak days. More infrequent now, but still like a poisonous cloud that fell over her very soul. In those times Joan neither dressed nor ate. She drifted through the house as ghost-like as the scent of Roger's throat lozenges. Her late husband wouldn't have approved of the times when she gave in to despair and longing, so it was for him as much as for herself that she kept busy and tried to remain useful.

Today she planned on visiting Belle Hammer. As a member of the small Lake Stanmore community, the author was a bit of a celebrity and one of Joan's favourite writers. But, more importantly, she was a neighbour who'd had rotten luck. Homemade lamingtons weren't much, but they were Roger's favourite, and as he would have said, *Comfort food is nothing to sneeze at.*

With the tub of chocolate and coconut treats tucked under one arm, Joan picked up her keys and patted her pockets, making sure she had her phone and small torch. It was later than she would have liked to make the walk to her neighbour's house. Opening the back door to a shock of chilly evening air, she almost gave in to temptation and took the car. But the air would clear her head and sleep would come easier after a good stretch of the legs. Nodding to herself, she strode around the side of the house and across the front lawn.

The walk was pleasant enough despite the chill. Joan kept to the left, being mindful of the need to keep oncoming traffic in her sights. Not that there was much in the way of cars on Silver Gum Lane. In spring and summer there were more comings and goings, a smattering of tourists who'd wandered off the beaten track or visitors weaving in and out of local roads. But in winter the most she'd expect was the Hammers, either Belle's old Holden or her husband's sports car on the streets. And didn't that young man like to belt along! Joan made a clicking sound with her tongue and inched closer to the shoulder of the road.

From the trees a kookaburra let rip with a gale of laughter, winding up to a chattering crescendo sharp enough to wake the dead. Joan turned her head, trying to spot the bird, but the trees were so tightly packed that their tall shadows crowded out the light. The bird's laughter made her think of something her mother always said about a kookaburra's laughter in the late afternoon. *Laughing before the sky falls.* Joan shrugged deeper into Roger's jacket, which she supposed was her jacket now.

She passed Arthur Howell's driveway, noticing his mailbox was leaning drunkenly to the right. *Makes sense.* Catching herself in the unkind thought, she clamped her lips together and scurried on. Arthur was a drunk and what her mother would have called an alchy. But wasn't alcoholism a sickness just like any other harmful compulsion of the mind and body? Maybe she should be bringing him the lamingtons. The poor bloke looked like he hadn't had a proper meal since Beijing hosted the summer Olympics.

Arthur was a tall bag of bones in a grubby raincoat, always loping from place to place, usually the bottle shop. Rena, at the little grocery shop in Stanmore Central, once told her Arthur used to be an English lecturer. The woman had more to say, but Joan shut down the gossip with a steely stare. A stare that could make milk curdle, that's what Roger called it. Joan didn't know how milk-curdling her stare was these days, probably more like a watery trickle than a flash of steel, but it was enough to quieten Rena's gossipy tongue.

Rounding the bend, Joan was pleased to see the lights on at the Hammer place. Calling before showing up would have been the polite thing to do, but she didn't have their number and intended to stay only long enough to deliver the lamingtons and make sure her neighbour was on the road to recovery. *And ask when her new book might be coming out.*

Joan chuckled to herself. It wouldn't hurt to ask a polite question about Belle's work.

Sensible walking shoes crunching up the driveway, a smile still lifting the corners of her mouth, she noticed a little white car, the sort of thing usually used by young girls, compact and on the cheap side. The vehicle was parked rather clumsily, almost at an angle. Joan slowed and took hold of the collar of her jacket. She hadn't thought about the possibility that the Hammers might have guests.

"Damn." This time she spoke to herself and not her late husband.

Night was drawing in, coming earlier each afternoon. The thought of walking home in the dark didn't really bother her, not when she had the torch. But still, it was getting late and she needed to make a decision before hesitation became loitering. Turn back and avoid intruding on the couple and their guest or push on and be a good neighbour?

"Should have come at lunchtime." As she spoke it occurred to her that turning up so late was a bit odd.

Joan looked down at the plastic tub, wondering what had possessed her to stalk through the late evening on such a feeble mission. In truth she'd made the cakes on impulse, only deciding to take them to Belle as an after-thought. Like all the other pointless things she now did, such as her online book club or volunteering at the senior's centre, baking was another exercise in feeling useful.

"Oh, for God's sake." She shrugged off her moment of anxiety and walked around the car, noticing it was in need of a wash.

She'd met Belle a few times in Stanmore Central. They'd even chatted about books. On those occasions, Belle Hammer seemed down to earth and friendly – a little fragile, not physically, but emotionally. It was something in the writer's intense brown eyes, the brittleness of a woman holding back a well of emotions. It was a fragility Joan hadn't recognised until she lost Roger and saw that same look in the mirror.

It was the look in Belle's eyes that finally decided things and without further hesitation, she knocked on the door.

Chapter Thirteen

Belle stared open-mouthed at the bedroom door. The burst of outrage that welled up when Lea shoved her into the bedroom was fading and replaced by a growing sense of danger. The girl was unbalanced; this was now painfully clear. But what Belle couldn't fathom was the reasoning behind Lea's behaviour. What could the carer possible hope to achieve by keeping Belle captive inside her own home?

She worked on her fingernail, this time the pinkie. Maybe the girl hadn't hoped to achieve anything. If she was taking drugs or just unhinged, there might not be any clear thinking behind it. Belle tasted blood, but continued gnawing at the nail. Figuring Lea out wasn't as important as getting help. With the phone and modem gone, the only way to do that was by going for help herself.

But right now she was too scared to come out of her own bedroom, let alone hatch an escape plan. Belle pulled her finger out of her mouth and stared at the bubble of blood forming on the cuticle. She was afraid. No, more than afraid; the girl terrified her. But there was something else too: shame.

From the moment Lea arrived, Belle had let the younger woman bully her. Even before she'd become violent, Belle had allowed herself to be intimidated and ordered around. Now she was sitting in her room scared to anger a carer she was paying for with her own money. So daunted was she by the girl's aggression, that Belle sat immobilised. *It's like I'm a little girl again.* An image flashed in her mind: the man with the brown tooth, smiling down at her. No, she corrected herself. Not smiling, leering. *All on your own?* His voice was like a snippet from an old song playing in her ears.

She had no idea if the incident with the teddy was a real memory or something she'd seen on TV. Maybe even a story she'd read. The mind had ways of manufacturing memories; all it took was a suggestion. And right now her mind was pulled so taut, it wouldn't take much to tear open everything she'd worked so hard at keeping together.

A memory or a bad dream, it didn't matter. All that counted was getting help. She scanned the bedroom, looking for inspiration and her gaze fell on the crutches. Her car keys were near the front door; at least they were the last time she checked. And her car, newly repaired, was in the garage. The thought of getting to the car gave her another idea, one that was risky but might be her best chance.

Belle pulled the chair up close to the door and listened. There was no sound from the sitting room, but that didn't mean Lea wasn't still on the couch watching the door. While leaning forward and straining to hear, a sound caught her attention. Not from the sitting room, but from above. Belle's head jerked up. A twinge of pain ran across her bruised eye socket. The discomfort registered and with it came the realisation that Lea had gone upstairs.

This was Belle's chance. With no telling how long Lea would remain on the second floor, Belle couldn't let her fear hold her back. She grasped the doorknob and turned it, wincing at the almost inaudible squeak. Moving in a wheelchair, no matter how carefully one manoeuvred, was never without noise. Even the hiss of the wheels on the floorboards seemed overly loud in the silence.

Belle rolled into the sitting room, trying to look in every direction at once. Arthur's head turned her way. Wispy grey hair clung to his forehead as his chin jerked up. He seemed to be trying to tell her the girl was upstairs. Belle nodded and put a finger to her lips.

There was no denying the man gave her the creeps and he'd come to her home and tried to force his way in, but in light of Lea's behaviour, Belle didn't believe he had brought the knife. Now she came to think of it, the knife Lea showed her looked very much like one of the set they had in the kitchen. Still, trusting Arthur could be a risk.

A knot had formed on the man's forehead, angry and dark like an overripe grape. The gash had stopped bleeding, sealed by a globby looking wet scab. Belle grimaced. "I'm going to take out the gag, but no screaming." She heard herself and suppressed a surge of hysterical giggles because she'd sounded like a bad actor in a horror film.

The absurdity of the situation was lost on Arthur. He nodded, his strings of limp grey hair clinging to his ears. Belle had to bend at the waist to pull the scarf out of his mouth. As she did the stench of sweat and stale alcohol rolled off of him in a putrid wave. It occurred to her that instead of fearing Arthur, she should pity him. After all, wasn't he just a reflection of her own future if she continued to drink?

"I didn't do anything." He gagged and a string of saliva hung from his bottom lip. "I was just–"

"Shh." Belle glanced upwards. "Where's your phone?"

Arthur followed her gaze, staring up at the ceiling. His bloodshot eyes grew misty. "She forced tablets down my throat. I wasn't going to hurt anyone… I–"

"Arthur." Belle grabbed his shoulder. She believed what he was saying, but couldn't waste time discussing it. "Where's your phone?"

"She took it when you were asleep." He spluttered out a cough that threatened to turn into another bout of gagging. "I don't know where she put it."

She wasn't surprised. Getting hold of Arthur's phone had only been a vague hope. "Okay, it doesn't matter." She took hold of the cord knotted at his wrists. "I'm going to untie you so you can go for help."

He nodded and she noticed that a latticework of broken capillaries covered the man's nose. "Yes. Yes, I'll get you out of here. That's what I was trying to do." He sounded sincere, not at all unhinged.

Belle was only half listening as she tried to work on the knots, using her ragged fingernails. Over the sound of Arthur's heavy breathing and the blood pulsing in her ears, she heard something that made her hesitate.

"Someone's coming." Belle's voice was a whisper. "On the driveway."

Arthur tried to turn his head towards the door at the same time footfalls thumped down the stairs.

Belle let go of the cord and started wheeling towards the front door. She had no idea who'd be walking up the driveway so late, but didn't care. Whoever it was could ring the police and get an ambulance for Arthur. It was over. Her crazy twenty-four hours with Lea was at an end.

"Get away from the door." Lea's voice was breathless, most likely from running down the stairs.

Belle ignored her and kept moving, but the girl was fast. As Belle's hand reached for the door, Lea grabbed the chair and pulled her back, swinging her around in a tight arc.

Lea leaned down, her face so close Belle could feel her breath, hot and laboured, on her skin. "You'd better get yourself together." The girl's eyes were wide and unblinking. "If you say one word to whoever's out there..."

She straightened and grabbed the tin of pineapple from the hallstand near the entrance. "I'll drive this through their face."

A knock, light and sharp, rang out. But the menace in the carer's voice cut through Belle's desperation to get to the door. She had no doubt the girl meant what she was saying. Before Belle could answer, Lea bent and grabbed the scarf off the floor and shoved it back in Arthur's mouth. She held the can above the man's head and, for a second, Belle thought she was going to strike him again.

"Don't." Belle kept her voice low. "I won't say anything. Just don't hit him."

Lea lowered the can, but kept her eyes on Arthur. "Make a sound and I'll use this."

* * *

Waiting on the small porch, the idea that she was intruding took hold and Joan decided she would leave the questions about Belle's latest book for another time. It was almost fully dark now and with only a waning crescent moon, the driveway and small car were in shadows. From inside the house came the sound of muffled voices.

As the seconds ticked by with no response, Joan began to wonder if the writer and her guest might be hoping she'd give up and go away. After all, Belle had only met her a few times and their friendly exchanges could be explained as politeness on the author's part. Maybe she was overstepping the mark by turning up uninvited to make a neighbourly gesture, but rudeness was rudeness no matter what a person did for a living. Had Joan, in her grief-cloaked mind, been mistaken about Belle Hammer? Maybe the depth she thought she'd seen in the woman's eyes was merely a projection of Joan's own misery.

Feeling not so much foolish as disappointed, Joan decided to take the high road and leave the lamingtons. As she untucked the plastic tub from under her arm, the porch light snapped on.

The door opened and a woman in a wheelchair appeared in the crack. Joan took in the woman's dishevelled appearance and battered face and hissed out a breath. Catching herself before shock fully registered on her face, she quickly arranged her features into a smile.

"Hello." Joan hoped the woman hadn't noticed her astonishment. For a moment the author simply stared, giving no indication of recognition.

"Hello." Belle's voice was husky, almost hoarse.

Sensing the need for further explanation, Joan pushed on. "I'm Joan... Joan Crow." She jerked a thumb over her shoulder. "I live at the end of the lane."

Only one of the author's eyes was visible, the other was hidden behind a limp and crinkled patch. From her position above Belle, Joan watched as recognition dawned on the woman's face. "Oh, yes." Belle raised a hand and rubbed her temple; the other she kept clamped on the door. "Sorry. My vision's not that great."

Joan waved a dismissive hand. "Don't apologise. It's my fault, taking you by surprise this late in the evening." She waited a beat, but when the author didn't respond, Joan pushed on. "I just wanted to drop by and ask how you're feeling." Joan held the tub out. "I made you some lamingtons... I thought a little treat might, you know..." Joan could feel her smile tightening. "I thought they might cheer you up." The last part came out sounding strained. When Belle made no move to take the tub, Joan wondered if she should dump it in the woman's lap.

Before she could decide how to proceed, the door jerked out of Belle's grasp and a young woman appeared behind her.

"Hi. I'm Lea." The girl looked no older than twenty-five and pretty in a sort of plain looking way. "I'm Mrs Hammer's carer."

Joan felt her face relax and her smile become a little less frozen. "Oh, I see." She held out the tub. "I was just dropping these off. I'm Joan from down the lane."

The girl took the tub and clasped it against her slim frame. "Thanks, we'll enjoy these." She looked down and addressed the top of Belle's head. "Won't we, Mrs Hammer?"

It struck Joan that the caregiver spoke to Belle slowly and with the sort of over cheerful tenor one might use on the very old or the very young. But Belle seemed unaware of the tone, giving a nod, but didn't speak.

"I was just helping Mrs Hammer to get ready for her shower." The girl jiggled the tub, making the lamingtons bounce. "Thanks for dropping by." There was finality in the way she spoke and Joan got the impression she was being dismissed.

"All right. Good." The girl regarded her with wide, questioning eyes. "I'll let you get back to it then." Joan took a step back. The situation felt awkward and she wanted very much to get away from the two women, but something stopped her.

"Is Mr Hammer home?" She'd never met Belle's husband and had only ever seen him from a distance or whizzing around in his sports car. But it seemed to Joan that Belle might need more than a shower. Her face looked gaunt and her hair, once long and bouncy, was now cropped and standing in messy spikes. While she knew the woman had been in a serious car accident, it didn't explain the look on the author's face. Joan didn't know her very well, but something felt amiss.

At the mention of her husband, Belle's one visible eye blinked rapidly. "No." Lea continued, speaking for her employer. "He's away for work." There was an edge to the girl's voice, cheerfulness, but tinged with irritation.

"Oh, right. Yes, well, if you need anything I'm down the lane." Joan pointed south. "Mine's the last house after Arthur Howell's place."

Maybe it was the shadows thrown by the porch light or it could have been Joan's imagination, but at the mention of Arthur's name, Belle's pale face turned a watery shade of grey.

"We have everything we need." As she spoke, the carer pulled Belle's wheelchair back from the door. "Good night." The girl balanced the tub on one of the chair's handles and flipped the door closed.

At a loss, Joan stood on the empty porch staring at the closed door. "I suppose that's what I get for being a busybody." She spoke quietly, imagining Roger shaking his head at the caregiver's insolence.

Before making the walk home, Joan pulled out the small torch stashed in one of her deep pockets and flicked on the switch. The light played over the white car, which she now supposed belonged to the carer. Not one to stay where she wasn't wanted, Joan stomped over the gravel driveway and headed back to her silent house. At least there she had her memories for company.

Chapter Fourteen

Lea let go of the chair and dumped the tub on the coffee table. Watching the girl move around the room with an air of authority caused a hollow feeling to take up residence in Belle's gut. Part of Belle, a small hopeful spark, wanted to believe Lea would get tired of whatever game she was playing and leave. But the carer had handled Joan with deftness and a sense of purpose that made everything that had happened seem more real. Lea wasn't fooling around.

"Who makes lamingtons?" Lea tore the lid off the tub and bit into one of the cakes. "It's like something out of the fifties." She spoke around a mouthful of chocolate and coconut.

The rich chocolaty smell reminded Belle she hadn't eaten since the previous evening. Suddenly hungry, she decided against anything as rich as Joan's cakes.

Moving past Arthur, it occurred to her that he needed food and water and probably a trip to the toilet. "Lea." Belle tried to sound casual. "I'm going to get something for Arthur to eat." She forced a joyless laugh. "I'm a bit hungry myself."

Lea turned from the tub with fingers coated in chocolate, then gripped the arm of the sofa. "Stop pretending to be such a saint." A spray of crumbs flew out of the girl's mouth. "You." She pointed a grubby finger in Belle's direction. "You're so selfish you make me sick."

Lea's usually blank face became flushed and her brows drew down in an angry V. She stood and let the tub tumble onto the rug. Belle moved back, trying to edge closer to the kitchen.

"I didn't mean anything." Belle tried to keep the panic out of her voice, but the caregiver's lightning fast, shifting mood was frightening to watch. "I just thought he might need something to eat."

Lea bent and scooped up a cake from the rug. "Oh, yeah. Good idea, Belle." She dashed around the sofa and flopped onto the floor next to Arthur. Belle saw Arthur wince and try to draw away. Watching him bound and helpless, for the first time since the crazy nightmare began, Belle experienced a spark of anger.

"Here you go, you old weirdo." Lea pulled the gag out of Arthur's mouth and shoved the cake in, her palm hitting his lips with a wet slap. She twisted her palm, smearing chocolate across the man's chin as his head twisted out of her grasp.

"Stop it." Belle wheeled forward, meaning to grab Lea's arm and yank her away.

Halfway across the room she heard Arthur gagging. "You're crazy!" His voice was gravely, but at the same time loud enough to make both women stop moving. "I saw you on the road. What did you do?"

"Shut up, you dirty alchy." With her head turned in Arthur's direction, Belle couldn't see the girl's face, but the fury in Lea's voice was enough to get Belle moving again.

As she reached the sofa, the carer grabbed the sides of Arthur's head and jerked it forward. "No, don't." Belle sprang forward in her chair and snatched at the girl's shirt.

Instead of grasping fabric, her fingers merely skimmed Lea's shoulder. Before Belle could try again, the girl slammed Arthur's head against the floor with a meaty thud. The man's legs splayed outwards. A damp patch appeared at his groin, spreading like a dark flood, turning his pants from light grey to a shade closer to black.

The moment stretched out, almost too grim to be real. Belle felt the strength seep out of her arms. Her head drooped. Inside, a scream was building, but the effort of letting it out seemed more than she could muster.

When Lea stood, Belle was struck by a new odour: urine. The sharp scent mixed with Arthur's sweat to create a thick stench that hung in the air.

"Happy now?" The caregiver spoke with indifference, the throw-away line so lacking in guilt or emotion that Belle wished she could stand and hit the younger woman, then grab her by the shoulders and force her to stare into Arthur's slack face. Never prone to violent thoughts, Belle clenched her fists, holding back the urge inside her to strike out.

Lea strode out of the room, leaving Belle to watch helplessly over Arthur's lifeless form. His eyes were closed and his mouth agape. Belle wheeled closer and dipped her head, listening for signs of life as the girl's footfalls thumped on the stairs. At first Belle could hear nothing above her own sharp breaths. She pressed her fingers to the man's throat, pushing against his skin. After a few attempts, Belle located his pulse. He was alive, but rather than a steady throb, Arthur's pulse was faint, an intermittent patter.

"Arthur?" She touched his shoulder, but didn't shake him for fear of causing further damage. "Arthur, can you hear me?" His eyelids remained closed, but his lower lip moved.

He needed help. Urgent help. Belle didn't know much about medicine, but he'd had two head injuries in the space of one day. There was no more time for sitting around biting her nails; she had to act.

Belle pushed her way to the front door. Her keys were in the bowl. Maybe Lea hadn't noticed them or thought

Belle was too helpless to use them. She grabbed them and stuffed them in her pants pocket. Overhead, a door slammed. The carer was in the bathroom.

It took Belle less than a minute to get into her bedroom and retrieve the crutches. With the sticks balanced across the arms of the wheelchair, she reached up and flicked on the porch light.

"Okay." Belle took a final look at Arthur and opened the front door.

The night air was a welcome shock, washing the stench and fear away with a blast of eucalyptus tinged wind. Belle used her shoulders, still well-muscled from years of daily laps, to push over the doorstep and onto the porch.

Unlike the rear of the house, the porch was level with the driveway. Belle didn't have to worry about navigating a slope or steps. Before moving she twisted in the chair and pulled the door closed, hoping the metallic whisper of the latch didn't alert Lea of her movements. Taking a deep gulp of fresh air, Belle put her good foot on the ground and pushed up off the wheelchair. Standing was easy. Crossing the gravel driveway would be the difficult part. *No. Getting away before my insane caregiver catches me and pounds my head into the ground is the hard part.*

Lea could be on her way downstairs and it wouldn't take long before she realised Belle had left the house. The girl's belief that her prisoner was too feeble to escape would buy Belle some time, but not much. With only minutes to spare, Belle took her first step only for her plan to fall apart. Lea's car was parked at an angle, blocking the driveway. With a half-metre ditch on the far side of the gravel strip, going around wasn't an option. Even if Belle made it to the garage and managed to get to her car, she'd never get past the girl's vehicle.

"Fuck." Belle leaned to her left and felt the crutch slip under her weight. The rubber stopper on the end of them had moved less than a few centimetres, but it was enough to make her heart stutter.

Lea was insane. Her moods shifted with violence and unpredictability, yet somehow everything seemed to go the girl's way. Maybe Belle was over-simplifying the situation. Everything the girl did seemed random and opportunistic, but maybe Lea was always a step ahead because she'd planned on taking Belle captive right from the moment she parked her car. It made no sense, but nothing about Lea made sense.

"Okay." Belle gripped the crutches in her fists. Her right leg was already struggling even with the added support of the sticks. "Now what?"

She took a wobbly step closer to the white car and the forward move helped ease the stress on her good leg. A little further from the house Belle tried to ignore the ache in her knee and think. It would be easy to hobble back to her wheelchair and go inside. The idea of locking herself in the bathroom came to mind.

It wasn't much of a plan, but better than nothing. As the idea took hold it occurred to her that she could drag something into the bathroom and barricade the door. At least she'd have water and the toilet. It was Sunday and no one was due to visit until Tuesday when her physiotherapist came. *Guy will send help. Bethany won't wait long before calling the police.* She might be able to wait the girl out by sitting tight until Lea gave up and drove away. Belle clamped the right crutch against her body and tried to wipe the sweat from under her glasses. But what about Arthur? How long could he last? Why the hell did Arthur have to show up?

As her mind skipped from one thought to the next, the minutes ticked by. Hiding in the bathroom might buy her some time, but at what cost to Arthur? She could live with taking the coward's way out, but she couldn't let a man die so she'd be safe. With no time left to dither, Belle made the decision to keep going and find a way to get help.

Taking another unsteady step, she made it to the rear of Lea's car. The only light came from the porch, not quite falling as far as the vehicle. But because of the car's pale colour, Belle could see most of it clearly enough. Belle leaned her body against the boot and let out a shuddering breath. How long had she been outside? It couldn't have been more than two minutes.

She glanced back at the front door. Any second now it would swing open and Lea would come charging out. Belle's only option was getting to the road. On crutches and wearing slippers, her chances of success were slim, but what else could she do?

She didn't need the ache in her leg to tell her painkillers had well and truly worn off. As much as she longed for the hazy tranquillity of her medication, she was grateful for the clear-headedness. If she stood any chance of survival, she needed to be able to think. She let her hand rest on the cold steel of the boot. If only she had Lea's keys.

The idea came like a thunderclap. The driveway sloped downwards towards the road. If the car was unlocked, she could put it in neutral, disengage the handbrake, and gravity would take care of the rest. Belle's heart fluttered at the idea, partly out of sheer terror, but mostly with excitement.

Now she was thinking again, using her mind to formulate a plan instead of calming her brain through endless counting. If the car was unlocked, the boot would be open and she could grab a tyre iron. That way if Lea came out of the house, at least Belle could fend her off.

"Yes," Belle muttered, not really aware she was speaking. "We'll have a catfight on the driveway." The idea was so gut-wrenching it made her want to giggle or sob; she wasn't sure which.

Balancing her weight on the crutches, she slid her fingers into the release and to her surprise the boot sprang open. The smell hit her before she could raise the lid. A sweet odour like raw meat mixed with cheap perfume. Belle gagged and tried to cover her mouth, an involuntary movement to ward off the stench that now filled her lungs.

As she moved, the boot flew up and her left crutch slipped forward and out of her grip.

Toppling forward, she put out her left hand but couldn't stop herself tipping into the boot. Like falling into a bloody nightmare, Belle's hand landed on something rigid and cold. The boot light was on and close-up the starkness of the dead body was inescapable. She took in the image in snaps that came fast and sharp as her eye blinked in the scene.

Belle let out a sound that sounded animal-like, and then she scrambled back, her fingers digging into hard, dead flesh and slipping into something sticky.

"Oh, Jesus." She wailed out a cry and steadied herself on the rim of the boot.

Wanting to back away but unable to move, she took in the horror. A girl, dead and folded on her side. Belle's one eye, although misty and almost closed, stared into the depths of the car at the dead girl's throat that had a thick piece of tree branch stuck through it. It took Belle a second to understand how a branch could be in the girl's neck. With that realisation came a gush of bile.

Belle vomited onto the girl's leg, a thick string of liquid that splashed on the corpse's navy pants. Groaning, Belle reached up to cover her face and realised her left hand was coated with something dark. Another spasm gripped her gut, twisting her stomach like trying to tear it into two.

"Get away from that." The voice cut through the immediate horror and Belle spun on her good foot.

Lea jammed her hand into Belle's armpit and squeezed, using her free hand to slam the boot down. Fighting back, Belle pushed at the girl, leaving a smear of dark blood on the caregiver's chin.

"You crazy bitch." Belle couldn't stop the words even if she wanted to. "You did that. You killed her. You… You. Get your hands off me." She was breathing hard, struggling to keep her balance and fight the girl off at the same time.

Lea's teeth were clenched, her lips pulled back with the effort to keep hold of Belle's armpit. In the near dark, the girl's eyes looked black. Without warning, she pulled back and slapped Belle with enough force to rock her head to the left. Some of the air went out of Belle's lungs and with it her strength ebbed.

"Get inside." Lea bit the words off like angry sparks.

She jerked Belle towards the porch. With only one crutch, Belle had no choice but to be marched back to the house. When they reached the wheelchair, Lea stopped.

"Get in." She pointed at the chair, but Belle pulled back. "Get in or I'll kick your knee out from under you." Lea's eyes, still black under the shadow of the porch, loomed close to Belle's face.

She wanted to resist. Every nerve in her body itched to pull away and run, but there was no mistaking the menace in the young woman's voice. Belle had seen what she was capable of. Running was out of the question. She let her head drop and hopped to the side, then slumped into the chair. Without another word, Lea pushed Belle back into the house as Belle counted the hiss the wheels made with each revolution.

Arthur was still unconscious, the only movement coming from his shallow breathing. The chair jolted as the carer swung around the sofa. Belle fixed her gaze on her hands. One coated in blood and the other with nails bitten past the quick. A few minutes ago she'd been determined to escape and get help. Now that determination had turned into helplessness. *It always comes back to helplessness.* Was there ever a time in her life when she wasn't a victim?

"I suppose you think you have me all worked out?"

Lea was speaking, but Belle was trying to reconcile what she'd seen in the boot and what that meant for her and Arthur. Death she supposed. Lea couldn't let them go now, not after what she'd done to Arthur and to the girl in the boot.

"Hey." Lea snapped her fingers close to Belle's injured eye. The sound made Belle jump. "I'm talking to you."

Belle's head felt heavy or maybe her neck was weak. Lifting her chin so she could meet the girl's gaze became an effort. Under the sitting room lights, the carer's eyes were blue and shining with intensity. She was watching Belle, waiting for something.

"You killed that girl, didn't you?" Belle didn't wait for an answer. "She had the same uniform as the one you're wearing. She's Lea." Belle swallowed back a wave of nausea. "So who are you?"

Chapter Fifteen

There was very little to pack, a few T-shirts and some dirty underwear. Most of Guy's possessions were in the bathroom. After his phone call with Andy, he'd woken the girl in his bed. Her name he learned was Candi with an 'i'. After some fast talking and a promise to call her when he flew back to New Zealand, he managed to get her out the door. Now alone and with midnight approaching, he scooped up his collection of skin care products, and dumped them in his shaving bag.

The bathroom was spacious with floor to ceiling marble tiles and a triple jet shower. Nice set-up, but probably the last he'll see of such luxury. His phone shrilled from the bedroom and for the first time in hours, he thought of Belle. She'd asked him to do something, but the headache he'd woken up with that morning had grown from a buzz into a drill and his thoughts were stilted and as bleary as his eyes.

Before zipping up the shaving bag, he rummaged around and found a strip of paracetamol. Popping two, he tossed them back with a handful of tap water. Scrubbing his hand over his mouth, he straightened up and despite his efforts to ignore it, the phone continued to peel out its strident call.

"Now what?" He answered without registering the number on the display.

"Guy?" At the sound of Belle's voice, relief floated out of the quagmire of misery he'd been wallowing in since lunchtime. He needed her, which was *one* thing about his life he'd never doubted. He'd leave this lonely place and go back to Belle; she knew how to make everything all right. He'd go back to her and find a way to make everything good again.

"Hi, babe. I miss you so—"

"No. No, sorry." She spoke rapidly now. "It's Bethany."

Guy's legs were unsteady. He let them fold under him and dropped back onto the bed. Belle's sister wouldn't be calling unless something was wrong. For a heartbeat, the hotel room vanished and he was back in his agent's office, back in the moment when he got the call about Belle's accident. "Bethany, what's wrong? Has something happened?" He had trouble catching his breath.

"No." Her voice was so like her sister's it was eerie. "I didn't mean to scare you. I know it's late in New Zealand, but I can't get hold of Belle and…" He could hear her taking a breath, steadying herself. "I just wondered if you'd spoken to her today."

He ran a hand through his hair, trying to remember the exact time he'd last spoken to his wife. "I talked to her at lunchtime." It was now close to midnight, so almost twelve hours ago. Why hadn't he thought to call her and check-in? "What time is it there?"

There was a pause before Bethany spoke. He could imagine her face, so like Belle's, only without the softness. Bethany would be judging him, counting the hours since he'd last spoken to his wife. His wife who was recovering from a serious accident.

"It's almost eight o'clock. I've been trying to get hold of her for a few hours, but she's not answering. I'm in Bali." There was an edge to her voice, not anger or judgement, but worry. The tightly contained panic in her words acted like a virus, jumping from her to him in lightning speed.

"Look, she's probably having a nap. She's on some heavy painkillers." He was careful to keep his tone calm for Bethany and himself. "She's got a caregiver with her, so if there was a problem she'd have called me." Everything he was saying made perfect sense, yet rationalising the situation didn't dispel the snake of fear that had curled itself around his lungs, making it difficult to keep the tremor out of his voice. "I'll hang up and call Belle. If I don't get hold of her, I'll ring our neighbour and send him over." He waited, but when his sister-in-law didn't answer, he pushed on. "Okay?"

Bethany sniffed, making him wonder if she'd been crying. "Okay, but ring me straight back." She sounded calmer now, but still upset.

There was a torn condom wrapper on the nightstand. Guy closed his eyes before he spoke. *Your wife's the one who's going to suffer and it will be your fault.* That's what Katrina had said. He still had the message on his phone. "I will." It was an effort to get the words out.

For a second he thought she'd hung up, but then she said something he knew she'd been holding back. "I never would have left the country if I thought you'd go off and leave her."

He opened his mouth to protest, to explain he'd had no choice and that he hadn't left her alone, but Bethany had hung up.

Before calling Belle, he went back over his messages, reading and deleting Katrina's texts.

* * *

Joan noticed the lights were out at Arthur's place. Even with a steep driveway, the glow from her neighbour's windows usually reached the road. It was odd for him to be asleep this early or out this late. But thoughts of Arthur and his comings and goings were fleeting, hardly registering as she grappled with something more pressing.

Leaving Belle's house, Joan had been reeling, at first with indignation before the emotions settled into something more painful. Her feelings were hurt. It was childish really, almost embarrassing. Not one for emotional displays, Joan sniffed back tears grateful that the road was dark and there was no one to witness her humiliation.

At the end of Arthur's driveway, she paused and stowed the torch under her arm, using her hands to push back her hair and drag a finger under each eye. She would have never believed grief would bring her this low, but the daily anguish was like a relentless master that directed her thoughts and emotions. Sorrow had become an almost tangible entity, sucking the joy and purpose out of life. Eighteen months ago, she'd gone to bed with the man she loved. No, Joan corrected herself. *I adored him.* Her lower lip trembled; the memory refused to be ignored.

Standing alone on the darkened road, Joan was no longer aware of the wind shifting through the trees or the cold air on her cheeks. She saw not the dark stretch of road, but sunlight spilling across a yellow bedspread. The sound of magpies yodelling out their morning song and Roger…

She closed her eyes and pulled the collar of her husband's jacket up around her throat. It *was* his jacket. It would always be his. Try as she did, she couldn't erase the image of him flat on his back with blank eyes staring upwards. The details of that last morning were so clear, the picture was jarring in its clarity. Small things: the way his pyjama top had ridden up on one side, revealing a patch of soft flesh on his belly; the stubble on his chin, grey with only a lingering fleck of black.

The cold worked its way under her clothes, touching her skin like phantom hands. Joan shivered and straightened her shoulders. These days it took so little to upset her.

"I'm all right, darling." She imagined Roger on the road ahead, his broad shoulders turned at an angle as the misty night surrounded him. "Just a wobble." She pulled the torch out from under her arms and walked on. "An old chook like me is allowed a little wobble."

As the memory slithered back to some jagged corner of her mind, something else surfaced and Joan frowned. Hurtful as the little scene at the Hammers' place had been, there were things that didn't sit right. All the emotions, the ups and downs of anguish, had almost washed away the disquiet that started when Joan looked at Belle Hammer.

Something was off. What that something was, Joan couldn't say. Her memory was still as strong as it had been twenty years ago, but what it was that bothered her was maddeningly beyond her grasp.

Still heading towards home, she decided to let the thought go. Experience had taught her that if something was worth remembering, she usually would remember it. "No use agonising over it."

Chapter Sixteen

Lea or the girl pretending to be Lea, propped Belle's crutch against the wall on the right of the front door. Then, moving with casual ease, she perched on the arm of the sofa. She wasn't quite smiling, but her face had taken on a countenance that suggested amusement. *She's enjoying this*, Belle thought, still waiting for the girl to speak.

"When I lost my foot, I thought my life was over." She shrugged. "And I was right, sort of. My old life, the one I cared about – that was gone." She reached down and pulled up the leg of her pants, revealing her prosthetic. "This is my life now."

For a moment the girl gazed at her artificial limb and appeared to be seeing it for the first time. "I remember every second of the accident." She looked back at Belle and the amusement vanished. "You know how people block out that sort of thing?" She didn't wait for an answer. "Not me. I'll never forget a second of what it felt like. I was leaving a party. The street was dark, only one light pole. I'd had a few drinks and something to take the edge off. I wasn't drunk, just a bit..." She lifted her hand and made an *either way* gesture. "I remember there was a footpath with a steep curb. It reminded me of that scene from "Singing in the Rain." You know when the guy's dancing on the sidewalk?"

Belle nodded, but didn't think the girl noticed. "I'd only flown back to Perth the day before and I was still on a high because I'd landed a part in an Off-Broadway show. A supporting role with a twenty-second dance solo." She wasn't looking at Belle anymore. Her eyes were fixed on something in the distance. Maybe she was seeing the memory play out in her mind. Belle wanted to interrupt, but decided to let the girl tell her story. Maybe talking through what brought her to do the unspeakable to the girl in the car would help her see she had to let Belle go.

"I was so excited that I started dancing." She smiled, an expression with such sadness that Belle could only watch and listen, a flicker of sympathy pulling her into the girl's story. "I was hopping on and off the curb, just like that guy in the movie." She started to hum, murmuring out a few notes and then stopped. "A car came around the bend. I heard it before I saw it. An old thing with one of those rumbling engines. I didn't take much notice because I was on the other side of the road, so I was safe, right?" She started humming again only this time with an intensity that bordered on anger. "I heard the car rev and then it was on top of me."

Lea closed her eyes. When she opened them she was staring at Belle. "It clipped me here." She tapped the artificial ankle." The driver would have barely felt it, but the wheel caught my bone and shattered it. That's what they told me later." Her voice was tight, as though holding back emotion. "At the same time, the rest of my foot spun around and was crushed against the curb. I felt every second, even the part when my flesh ripped off like an old sock."

Belle's hand went to her throat. "Jesus, Lea…" She didn't know what to say. Just imagining the pain was enough to make Belle's already fragile stomach churn.

"My name's Georgia," she said in an off-hand way before continuing. "I didn't pass out." She nodded. "Dancers are pretty tough. We have to be. We push through the pain." She pointed a finger in Belle's direction. "This is the funny part. The driver stopped. I was on the pavement by then, screaming for help. I saw the brake lights come on so I know the driver knew they'd hit me." She shook her head. "I had my hand like this." She wrapped her fingers around her prosthetic ankle. "Only instead of skin and bone, I felt mush and blood. That's when I really started to howl. The car drove away." Her voice dropped to little more than a whisper. "They drove away and left me screaming for help." She let go of her artificial limb and levelled Belle with an accusing stare. "You drove away."

* * *

Guy listened to the ringing. He was thousands of kilometres away, yet the sound was clear. On the fourth ring, he cursed loudly, only to bite back the word when the call connected.

"Hi, babe." His words came out in a rush of relief. "I was getting worried."

"Guy." Hearing his name on his wife's lips settled his nerves.

His initial relief turned to irritation, not at Belle, but at Bethany. As if things weren't bad enough without his sister-in-law getting him all cranked up. "Just wanted to check in and hear your voice."

"Oh, that's nice... I... I miss you." The emotion in her voice caught him off guard and with his bed still warm from another woman, his throat constricted.

"I miss you too." As he said the words, he realised how much he meant them. "I've been thinking about you. I shouldn't have left you." He rubbed his eyes and looked up at the ceiling. "The movie's a wash so I'm coming home."

"What?" She was surprised. He could hear it in her voice, but so was he. They'd both believed this was his big break. "What do you mean? When… I mean when will you be back?"

"Yeah. I know it's fucked up, but you know how these things go..."

"When will you be here?" There was an edge to her voice, demanding, almost shrill.

Guy tried to laugh away the awkwardness, but all that came out was a hoarse bark. "Relax, Belle. I'm okay with it. You shouldn't get upset. There'll be other movies." He tried to sound unconcerned, but he could hear the desperation in his own voice. "You're not pissed at me, are you?"

There was a pause. He could hear her breathing. He couldn't blame her for being angry. He'd gone off and left her when she really needed him and then he'd managed to blow the chance of a lifetime. It was a miracle that someone as good and kind as Belle put up with him. If she knew the things he'd done – if she knew what sort of a man he was she'd be disgusted. Hell, he was disgusted at himself.

"Belle?" He stood up and walked to the window. The city outside was a cross-work of lights swathed in blackness. The lights made him feel small and worthless.

"I'm not pissed." Her voice sounded stiff. "There's just things to sort out, you know with the girl from the agency. I'll need to tell her you're coming back." The words were tumbling out so quickly, he was having trouble keeping up with her. "She'll want to know when… when her job's finished. We can't just spring it on her. That wouldn't be fair."

"Okay. Okay." He turned back to the bed, checking the time. "If everything's on time with the flight, I'll be there by tomorrow lunchtime. But I don't see what the big deal is. I'll just pay her for the whole day."

"No. No, it's not a big deal." She sounded calmer now. "Okay, I'll see you tomorrow. I–"

"Hang on." Usually he was the one in a rush while Belle always wanted to talk, but now she seemed eager to finish the conversation. "Can you let your sister know you're okay? She's been trying to call you."

"Yes, yes, I will... I love you."

"I love you too and I..." He stopped, realising she'd hung up.

* * *

The girl, Georgia, ended the call and began flicking through the contacts. "What's your sister's name?"

Belle ignored the question. "You heard Guy. He'll be back tomorrow." She was playing for time, not wanting to give Georgia her sister's name. While Bethany was still worried, there was a chance she'd call the police. "I've told you I wasn't the one who hit you. I'd never do something like that, I swear. Why don't you just go before he gets back? If you go now, you can leave the State." Belle couldn't take her eyes off the phone and the way the girl's finger jabbed at the screen. "You could drive me to an ATM. I'll give you money and... and you can disappear."

"You'd like that, wouldn't you?" Georgia spoke without looking up. "I bet you wish you'd killed me instead of just taking my foot."

Still emotional after hearing Guy's voice, Belle slammed her hand down on the arm of the wheelchair. "I didn't hit you! Whatever you think happened, you're wrong."

Georgia looked up, a smile lifting the corners of her mouth. "Bethany?"

Belle's shoulders sagged. Bethany was her last chance, but now that small glimmer of hope had disappeared.

Georgia held the phone and began reading one of Bethany's last texts. "Hi, Sis." Her voice was breathless and overly cheerful. "My two boys have been in the pool all morning so I'm off to buy you a special gift. Here's a clue. It's something you wear and something you drink. Ha ha!" Georgia looked up over the top of the phone, her tone changing with her mood. "You're sister sounds like a moron."

Belle closed her eyes. Bethany sent the text two days ago and at the time Belle had laughed so hard she thought the wire in her knee might spring open. From anyone else, a T-shirt with a beer logo, even one Bali was famous for, would seem like a cruel joke when bought for a recovering alcoholic. But with Bethany, it was different. The two sisters shared a wicked sense of humour that was lost on everyone else. Even Guy couldn't understand why the two women thought their offbeat jokes were so funny.

With her cheek still stinging from the slap the girl gave her when they were outside, Belle bit off a response. "Irony's lost on someone like you." As soon as the words were out, Belle knew she'd gone too far.

Georgia's eyes widened and colour filled her cheeks. "What do you mean someone like me?" She slipped the phone in her pocket and took a step closer to Belle. "Well?"

Belle turned her wheels, trying to back away, but Georgia caught hold of the chair. The threat of violence was almost tangible, clouding the air like smoke. Belle could hear her heart thundering in her ears as the girl let go of the chair and balled her hands into fists.

It was madness to provoke the girl, but maybe insanity was catchy, because even though Belle knew it was reckless, she couldn't resist speaking her mind. "Someone like you?" Belle's voice was shaking, not with fear but anger. Anger for herself and for Arthur, but mostly for the girl in the boot. "You're insane. A killer. You could never understand how normal people communicate. You have no..."

Georgia struck, lips pulled back and teeth bared. She lifted her fist and pounded it down onto Belle's injured knee. The nylon brace on her leg hardly stifled the impact of the girl's blow. The pain was instant and white hot. Belle's head rocked back and she screamed, a long and tortured sound that tore at her throat. Her hand clamped over her patella while inside the floating bone it felt like a beehive alive with a thousand burning points of agony.

She wasn't sure if she lost consciousness or her vision merely dimmed, but suddenly there were grey spots clouding her eyes. The world, the sitting room, and Georgia disappeared until there was nothing but pain.

Chapter Seventeen

Joan settled on an omelette. She considered adding a glass of wine to her evening meal, but as her mother always said, *Wine should be for enjoyment, not mood control.* Drinking alone was sure to end in tears. She didn't need to look any further than her neighbour to see that truth play out.

Pushing the meal around her plate, Joan couldn't shake the feeling she was missing something. The mouth-watering mixture of fresh eggs, cheese, and green capsicum should have been enough to tempt her failing appetite, but the incident at the Hammers' house played over in her mind, making it impossible to give her attention to the food.

She scooped up a forkful of food and pushed it into her mouth, oblivious to the sweet, nutty flavour of gruyere cheese. It wasn't just one thing that was off about the encounter, there was a string of things. Small things that niggled away at her thoughts.

Mostly it was Belle's eye-patch. The gauze looked dirty and wrinkled; the tape peeling up at the edges. The patch needed changing. So why was it that neither Belle nor the caregiver seemed to notice?

Joan put her fork down and tapped a finger to her lips. She turned in her chair and looked out the kitchen window. It was fully dark now, but there was enough light from the house to see the jacaranda. In the wash of yellow light, the bare branches looked claw-like. Thinking about claws, something else came to mind.

Belle's fingernails. In her mind's eye, Joan could see the author rubbing her temple as though trying to massage her thoughts. Her nails were bitten. But bitten wasn't the correct word. Bitten would be normal enough. No, Belle Hammer's nails were gnawed. They were bloody at the edges and around the cuticles. It wasn't a big thing. The eye-patch wasn't a big thing either, but together the two smaller things were worrying and odd.

Staring intently at the window but not really seeing, Joan only noticed the set of yellow eyes when they moved closer. She didn't need to see the animal's soft brown fur to recognise the ringtail possum. The creature's reflective lenses amplified the light, giving the impression of huge yellow globes. Leaving the cover of the peppermint trees to venture close to the house was a bold move on the little marsupial's part.

"Careful, girl." Joan spoke aloud as though the possum could hear her through the glass. "There are foxes in these woods."

In response to Joan's voice, the animal's eyes darted left then right. She waited, expecting the possum to flee, but instead it continued to watch her. The idea of vulpine predators watching in the cover of darkness made Joan shiver and the girl's face, the one who introduced herself as Belle's carer, came to mind.

Joan dragged her gaze away from the possum and stood. Picking up her plate, she went to the fridge and stowed the food. Was she making more out of the incident because the girl had been rude to her? Or was it because the look in the girl's eyes worried Joan more than Belle's dirty eye-patch and ragged fingernails?

But there was more, something that had drifted on the edge of her thoughts since the walk home, a maddening wisp of information dancing just out of reach. The sensation was like walking into a room and forgetting what you were about to do. Standing with her hand on the fridge door, it came to her. The white car. When Joan turned on her torch just as she was about to walk away, the beam landed on the boot. What she'd seen hadn't struck her as unusual, not at the time, and not while she was reeling with hurt and embarrassment.

Now, staring at the fridge door, the smudge of mud she'd seen on the white car's back panel gave her pause. She'd given the vehicle no more than a passing glance. Red mud wasn't out of the ordinary, not in Western Australia where the land seemed to consist of white sand for a few kilometres back from the coast and then at some point morphed into red earth.

Joan turned from the fridge and scratched her head. She hadn't inspected the car, but didn't remember spotting mud on any other area. *I didn't even see the front of the vehicle. It could have been caked in mud.* Was it mud? Or was the mark she'd seen a smudge?

"Damn it." She twisted her wedding ring, turning it on her finger. "It was too dark to be mud. Mud would look orange, but the smudge was almost brown, like…" She couldn't quite bring herself to say it aloud.

Not saying it didn't change what she was thinking. Blood. Not mud, but blood. And not a smudge but a palm print. If she hadn't been so emotional, she'd have stopped and taken a closer look. But remembering the way her cheeks burned with shame and her eyes filled with tears still stung. She'd been disarmed, that was the word for the way she'd felt leaving the author's porch.

"It could have been blood." She was speaking to Roger now, imagining him at the sink, his head half-turned, one quizzical eyebrow raised.

She could almost hear his voice. "If you think it was blood, then do something about it."

Joan wanted to do something, but what? Still twisting the ring, she glanced out the kitchen window. The possum was long gone. But the little folivore made her realise that there were things, dangerous things that hid in plain sight. Like the foxes waiting for a possum to venture too far from the safety of the peppermint trees. Could that be what Joan had seen at the Hammers' house? Something sinister unfolding right in front of her?

The idea of calling the police came and just as quickly went. What would she tell them? Belle's dressing needed changing? There was a suspicious smudge on the car? No, the police would dismiss her as the local sticky-beak. She made a clicking sound with her tongue. If she had Belle's husband's number, she could call him. At least if she spoke to him and laid out her concerns, he could decide what to do.

She didn't have the man's number, but she knew someone who did. Not giving herself time to ponder, Joan grabbed Roger's jacket from the hook on the back door and slipped it on. This time she would take the car.

* * *

"Okay. Bethany just sent a pic." Georgia was talking, rambling on about text messages.

Belle raised her head, trying to focus on the girl's voice, but the pain in her knee was like a point of steel grinding into her leg. The caregiver had hit her hard, maybe even hard enough to tear the wire that held her patella together. Earlier she'd been desperate to escape and get help, but now all Belle wanted was relief from the pain.

"Can I have my pills?" Her throat was raw from the screaming, making it difficult to push the words out.

Georgia was perched on the end of the sofa. Behind her, the front window was black and cold. "No." Her voice was light, almost friendly. "No more painkillers for you." She stood and approached Belle's chair. "Here, this will cheer you up."

Belle's pulse kicked up a notch and she shrank back in the chair, using her hands to cover her knee. Georgia rolled her eyes and gave a sharp chuckle.

"I just want to show you the picture your sister sent." She stood a metre or so away and held out the phone.

There was a smudge on Belle's lens, but leaning her chin forward she was able to make out her sister's face, tanned and smiling. Jack grinned from Bethany's lap and behind them was what looked like a beachside restaurant. Her vision blurred and her sister's image became little more than a dark haze. For the first time since the nightmare began, it occurred to Belle that she might not ever see her family again.

Belle reached for the phone, but Georgia snatched it away. "Don't worry. I'll tell her she looks great." The girl pursed her lips and stared at the screen. "Although she really does look like a fat cow in that sarong."

A tremor ran through Belle's arms and shoulders. The pain was settling into a brooding ache, but her body was still jumpy with adrenalin. Moving slowly, trying not to jostle her knee, she turned the chair and headed for the archway.

"Where are you going?" Georgia's voice followed her.

"Water." Belle didn't have the strength or the desire to speak to the girl who was now her captor.

Listening, waiting for Georgia to race after her, Belle wheeled through the dining room and into the kitchen. When the girl didn't follow, Belle let out a shaky breath. Being alone, even if it was only in the next room, felt like a small measure of freedom.

Belle let her face drop into her hands, pushing her palms against her clammy cheeks. The girl was torturing her, punishing her for something she didn't do. After what Belle saw in the boot, she knew Georgia was capable of much worse. How long would it be before Belle ended up like the girl?

She took a bottle of water from the fridge and twisted off the cap. After swallowing a few mouthfuls, she held the bottle against her face, relishing the cold on her skin. The kitchen, though fairly spacious, seemed smaller; the cupboards overhead loomed too high and seemed ready to tip and crush her. For the second time that day she felt small and helpless.

All on your own? Why, with so much immediate danger, couldn't she get the man's voice out of her head? He wasn't real. The memory wasn't real. It couldn't be. But the sneakers were real. She remembered those red sneakers and how much she loved them. The way the gold ribbon sparkled. The *dab, dab, dab* of the rubber soles on the department store floor.

His hair looked slippery, greasy and curling around his collar. The car door creaked open and the man pushed her inside. There were squashed cans on the floor and an old towel on the back seat. The smell, like the gunk that her mother cleaned out of the tray at the bottom of the stove, it was in her mouth, making her cough and choke.

"Okay. Be real quiet now." His face growing bigger and slick with sweat.

She was crying – big hiccupping sobs that racked her chest until she had no breath left. There was blood. At first she thought it was from her knee, but then she could see it on his hands.

The water bottle in Belle's hand had grown warm against her face so she set it on the counter. Her chest was heaving as though she'd swam ten laps. Something was happening to her mind. It was the only tangible explanation for whatever these flashes were. *They're waking nightmares.* She'd just seen a dead body, the first dead body she'd ever laid eyes on. Was it any wonder her brain was having trouble coping?

She spun the chair around to face the dining room. The problem wasn't some half-remembered scenes from a movie. They were graphic, terrifying scenes that had wormed their way into her brain like a parasite. The problem was the crazy woman in her house. And, if she had any chance of getting through the madness that was unfolding, Belle needed to stay in the here and now.

She'd been in the kitchen too long. If she didn't get back in the sitting room soon, Georgia would come looking for her. Belle scanned the room, taking in the dirty dishes on the table and the pile of crockery in the sink. The room was starting to smell like rotting fruit. The carer had been in her house less than twenty-four hours and everything was descending into chaos.

The plan to lock herself in the bathroom was beginning to seem like her only option. But that still left Arthur. Belle raked her fingers across her scalp. What could she do? The now familiar feeling of hopelessness welled up and with it, unwanted memories again threatened to surface.

"No." Belle thumped her fist on the arm of the chair.

She wasn't helpless. Yes, her leg and eye were injured, but she was a strong and resourceful woman when she wasn't drunk or paralysed by anxiety. She had two arms and a keen mind; it was time to use them.

Spinning the chair, she yanked open the drawer next to the sink. She could take a knife from the chopping block on the counter, but if Georgia was observant she'd notice one was missing. Instead, Belle settled on a smaller knife from the cutlery drawer and shoved it in her pocket.

On her way back to the sitting room she heard a thud overhead and realised the girl was upstairs again. With no time to waste, she pistoned her arms, picking up speed.

Arthur had moved. The cord around his ankles had come loose and one of his legs had stretched away at a forty-five-degree angle. She hoped that was a good sign. Belle leaned over and touched the man's shoulder. "Arthur. Arthur, wake up." His lids fluttered then opened.

"Yes." Belle clasped the lapel of his raincoat. "That's it. Come on, Arthur. I need your help." She tore at the knots, loosening the cord at his wrists. "I'm untying you."

His eyes, unfocused and dreamy, reacted to her voice and, for a second, he was looking up at her. But no sooner had he locked onto her gaze, his lids drooped and closed. Belle let out a curse and sat back in her chair. Dragging him was impossible. The man was skinny, but at least six feet tall. Unconscious, he was dead weight.

"Okay." Georgia spoke from the archway. "Time is getting away from us and we really need to talk." Belle glanced over her shoulder and saw that the girl had a bottle in her hand. She held up her hand with the palm flat. "Don't go anywhere." Her voice was cheery as though entertaining guests. "I'll get some glasses."

The caregiver headed back through the dining room. Belle turned back to Arthur. "For Christ's sake, wake up." She hesitated, her hand just above his face, and then she gritted her teeth and gave the injured man a sharp slap on the cheek. "Arthur."

His eyes opened. "I brought you a fig branch." His words were slurred, but understandable.

Belle grasped his coat and pulled. "What? I don't know what you're talking about." She gave his lapels a shake. "Listen, next time she goes upstairs I need you to move. We have to lock ourselves in the bathroom." Leaning so close to his ear, she almost tipped out of her chair as she whispered. "If you can't move, I'll have to leave you." A sob caught in her throat, making it difficult to go on. "Please, Arthur. I can't do this on my own."

"What are you whispering?" Georgia came up behind her, glasses clinking as she approached. "I told you before to keep away from him."

Fearing the girl was about to lash out, Belle wheeled back from Arthur and turned her chair. "Sorry." She gave the caregiver a worried look. "I was just checking his pulse."

Georgia tipped her head to the left and tightened her jaw. "Yeah, cause you're so concerned about others." She jerked her chin towards the sofa. "Get over there."

Belle nodded and pushed away from Arthur. She gave the girl a wide berth, positioning herself on the far side of the coffee table.

"Right." Georgia slammed the glasses down on the coffee table and kicked the cake tub, sending a half-eaten lamington bouncing across the rug. She held the neck of the vodka bottle and waved it in Belle's direction. "Let's have a drink. We've got lots to talk about."

Chapter Eighteen

The headlights splashed the ramshackle building with bluish light, turning Arthur's house a ghostly grey. Joan turned off the engine and climbed out of the car. Within seconds, the Toyota's interior light snapped off, dropping the house and surrounding bush into darkness. After a moment scrambling through the jacket's deep pockets, she located the torch and turned it on.

"Oh, Arthur." The words came out with a puff of warm breath.

The house was worse than she'd expected. Although she wasn't sure what she'd find at the end of her neighbour's driveway, Joan wasn't prepared for the run-down wreck. Two windows stared out from beneath a collapsing porch. The pane on the left had been smashed. Shards of jagged glass clung to the frame, which was now blocked by a sheet of red board.

She stepped onto what she thought had once been a flagstone pathway now overgrown with damp weeds, and picked her way towards the building. Shining the torch's beam to the right, she spotted Arthur's old Volkswagen sitting beside a row of old milk crates. In the darkness, the stacks of empty bottles piled in the crates twinkled like fairy lights.

There was sadness in this place. Before losing Roger, Joan would have thought herself to be the least mawkish person she knew. But circumstance and experience had softened her. Or maybe grief opened a person up to emotions that others kept hidden. Whatever the reason, she felt the wretchedness of the property's owner like a physical weight. *Is this how my home seems to strangers?* No, she was careful to keep up appearances. Her sorrow was clothed in a spotless home and well-maintained gardens.

Stepping onto the porch, the boards groaned as if unused to the weight of the living. Joan shivered. She should be at home preparing for bed, her feet in warm slippers, a good book in her lap, and a soft but empty bed waiting. Not out here in the cold, most likely sticking her beak where it didn't belong. She was being impulsive, worrying over something that might be nothing and yet she couldn't get the image of Belle out of her mind: her fingers bleeding and a dirty dressing on her eye, while the girl hovered over her with fox-like sharpness in her eyes.

Shining the torch on the front door, Joan raised her chin and stepped forward. She gave a sharp knock, hoping it was loud enough to raise Arthur from an alcohol-induced slumber. Not surprised when he didn't respond, she made a fist and thumped on the door hard enough to make the old wood shudder.

After another round of pounding, she stopped. It was no use; he was obviously out cold. Maybe it was the universe's way of telling her to give up and go home, but Joan wasn't ready to quit, not yet. She pressed her lips together and grabbed the doorknob. To her surprise it turned and the door swung inwards with a lazy creak.

Rather than entering, she leaned her head into the room. "Arthur?" Her voice was overly loud in the silent house. "Arthur, it's Joan from down the lane."

She hovered in the doorway, listening for movement. It occurred to her that her neighbour might be dead. Roger's face, eyes half open but misty and devoid of life flashed in her mind and her hand, still clamped on the doorknob, trembled. If Rena at the grocery shop hadn't been so sure that Arthur and Guy were unlikely friends, Joan would have turned and ran like a rabbit.

"Arthur." There was a quiver of panic in her voice as it reverberated into the dark building.

Standing on the doorstep yelling was doing any good. If she meant to help Belle, Joan would have to venture inside and shake Arthur awake so she could get Guy's number. Shining the torch around the doorway, she located a light switch and flicked it on.

The small but neat sitting room was a surprise. Somehow in her mind, Joan had imagined the interior of Arthur's house would be as dishevelled as his appearance. But instead of piles of clothes and empty bottles, the sitting room was spotlessly clean. While the sofa, bookcase and recliner were worn, they were still functional and tidy.

The smell was a different matter. Joan wrinkled her nose at the powerful odours of cheap wine and mildew that hung in the air. Looking around the space, she became aware of the damp spots creeping their way down the corners of the room. Like the outside, the living area was in need of repair. But no matter how pitiful they were she wasn't here to solve Arthur Howell's living arrangements.

There was an archway at the rear of the room. Venturing a few metres into the sitting room, she could see it led to an empty kitchen. Her only other option was a closed door on the left. She approached the door, hoping to hear snoring or some sounds of life from the other part of the house.

With still no detectable noise, Joan opened the door and peered down the dim hallway. "Arthur?" Becoming increasingly nervous, she raised her voice until it was close to a bellow. "Arthur Howell, wake up!" Her words bounced off the walls, sounding flat and out of place.

Light from the sitting room did little to chase the gloom away, so she played the torch's beam around the hallway. The light picked out three doors. *This is getting crazy.* Impatience was beginning to replace nervousness. It was Arthur's business how he lived his life, but this level of drunkenness was beyond the pale.

Emboldened by irritation, Joan strode to the first door and flung it open. Like the sitting room, Arthur's bedroom was neat, clean and shabby. It was also empty. The double bed was made, a washed-out blue bedspread neatly tucked with hospital corner precision over the thin mattress. Apart from a wardrobe, bedside table, and dog-eared book, the room was bare.

Joan stared at the bed certain that she was missing something. The dented mattress and worn book told a story. This room, like the rest of the house, appeared to be lived in, yet if this was Arthur's bedroom where was its owner? His car was in the driveway. Surely a man like Arthur wouldn't be out walking on a winter's night.

With two other rooms still to check, she backed out of the bedroom. The second door opened onto a small bathroom, again neat but shabby. At the final room, she hesitated. *If he's dead, I'll pull myself together and call the police.* A great plan if she could work up the courage to open the door.

Before entering, Joan gave a polite knock. "Arthur?" Not waiting for a reply, she flung the door open and snapped on the light. What she saw took her breath away and for a moment she could only stare.

* * *

"Here." Georgia sloshed vodka in both glasses before pushing one across the coffee table.

Far from being odourless, the vodka bombarded Belle's sense of smell. For a few seconds, she could only stare at the glass and imagine what the liquid would taste like as it hit her tongue. How the first gulp always made her shiver and then the sense of release that came from knowing the world was about to soften.

Georgia lifted her glass, but didn't drink. "I knew it was you." She kept her eyes on the clear liquid, studying its translucent qualities as she spoke. "Not right away. For a long time I had no idea who stole my life." She smiled, but her expression held no humour or joy. "But then I saw that article in Woman's World." She took a sip and grimaced. "At home with Australia's own Belle Hammer. What a load of shit." The bitterness in the young woman's voice dragged Belle's attention off her untouched drink. "I saw that picture of you, trying to pretend you were shy. But what really got me was the car." She jabbed a finger in Belle's direction. "What did it say? Oh, yeah. I remember." She lowered her voice and leaned forward. "The only thing the talented writer loves more than her husband is her vintage Holden. Bam." Georgia slammed her hand down on the arm of the sofa and Belle jumped.

"It was one of those moments." She clicked her fingers next to her ear. "A light bulb moment. Only instead of a light bulb mine was a detonation." She took another sip and set the glass down. There was a light in her eyes, glassy and urgent that made Belle's heart jump a beat. "I recognised your car and it was like a sign." She waved her arms upwards. "Like the universe had shined a light on you and... And..." Georgia balanced on the edge of the sofa, her knees bumping the coffee table. "I knew I had to make you pay for what you did to me. If I went to the police, I literally wouldn't have a leg to stand on." Laughter, shrill and forced, bubbled out of the girl's mouth. "Come on, that's funny." Her brows shot up in mock surprise. "No, you don't think that's funny?"

"I didn't do it." Belle glanced down at her glass, but made no move to pick it up. "There are lots of old Holdens out there. Whoever hit you...it wasn't me."

Belle clenched her fists and clamped them in her lap, waiting for the girl to explode into anger or violence. But to her astonishment, Georgia didn't seem to register Belle's denial.

"The article said you lived in the south west near Yallingup so I did some research." Georgia picked up her glass and took a long swallow, almost draining it. "I followed your Facebook page, searched old articles about you. It didn't take much to track you down to Lake Stanmore. The hardest part was waiting around, watching your routine."

Belle could feel sweat gathering on the back of her neck. As the girl prattled on, Belle had a sinking feeling in the pit of her stomach, like being on a high-speed elevator plummeting towards ground level.

"I used my uncle's old jeep." She wiggled her fingers in the air, making quotation marks around the word *uncle*. "He's not my real uncle. Just the guy my mother's shacked up with. He's always had a soft spot for me. A real soft spot." There was something sinister in the way she talked about her mother's partner, making Belle wonder if the girl had been through something traumatic with the man. *All on your own?* That voice, the greasy hair; Belle rubbed her temple, trying to dislodge the image from her mind.

Had Georgia been abused by her mother's boyfriend? The very thought of it set Belle's heart rate soaring with a mixture of pity and fear. But then she recalled the crack as Arthur's head hit the floor and saw the stick caked in blood and gore protruding out of the girl's neck in the boot. Whatever experiences Georgia had endured, it didn't excuse what she'd done.

"See, I knew my uncle wouldn't make a fuss if I brought the Jeep back all smashed up. He's got a mate that runs a scrap yard, so it's easy for him to get rid of a car." The girl snatched up the bottle and poured herself another drink. "Don't feel like drinking?" She jerked the bottle towards Belle's glass.

Not trusting herself to speak, Belle shook her head. The carer hesitated, her eyes scrutinising Belle's face. She seemed about to say something but shrugged instead.

"When I rammed your car I thought I'd killed you, but then it was on the news about you recovering in hospital." She picked up her glass and took a sip. When she spoke, the casual air had evaporated, replaced by a grittiness. "Yeah, it was a big deal when you had an accident. What happened to me didn't even rate a mention."

Georgia was angry and after what Belle had witnessed, the girl could be unpredictable. She didn't want to do anything to provoke the girl, but if what she was saying was true, Belle's accident was anything but. Suddenly the weeks of pain and the indignity of being handicapped were crowding in on her, piling up until she felt like she'd suffocate on the anger if she didn't let it out.

"You did this to me?" Her voice was a shriek. "You're…" She tried to think of something cruel enough – something that would wipe the smirk of satisfaction off the girl's face. "You're a lunatic." But instead of hurting Georgia, Belle's words seemed to please her. "You're a freak." The girl's grin melted into shock. *Good.* "You're a one-legged monster."

As soon as the words were out, Belle regretted their ugliness. Before she could say anything Georgia was on her. Pushing the coffee table aside, the girl lunged at Belle and grasped her around the neck.

Georgia's fingers closed around Belle's throat, her thumbs pressing on her windpipe. Belle's first instinct was to grab the girl's shirt and try to push her away. But Georgia was above her using her weight to push down. Straining back, desperately pulling away from the carer's hands, Belle twisted her head left then right but couldn't break free.

"You bitch." Spittle sprayed out of Georgia's mouth, showering Belle's cheeks as the girl's eyes seemed to grow into huge dark wells.

Belle's lungs burned from lack of oxygen. Her eyes watered, turning Georgia into a blur of movement and curses. She'd given up trying to push the girl away. Instead, she clawed frantically at the hands squeezing the soft tissue of her neck. A circle of light bloomed in Belle's functioning eye and she could feel the strength draining out of her arms.

With the will to fight still strong, Belle dropped her right hand into her lap and fumbled for her pocket. The spot of light in her eyes turned dark and for a split second, the room dimmed. When her fingers closed on the knife, Belle doubted she'd have the strength to lift the small utensil.

"You don't deserve to live, you selfish cow." Georgia's breath, heavy with the stench of alcohol, bathed Belle's face.

Moving blindly and on instinct, Belle rammed her right hand upwards. Georgia screamed, the sound so close to Belle's ear, the noise felt like it was coming from inside her head. Heat and moisture washed over Belle's hand. But at that moment nothing mattered beyond sucking air into her lungs.

The pressure on Belle's throat vanished and a trickle of air scraped past her swollen throat. She coughed and inhaled then gagged as cold air like shards of ice stung her windpipe. Warm tears dripped down her cheeks and her chest contracted in violent spasms. All the while, Belle clutched the knife, holding it out in front of her in a shaking hand.

She could hear heavy breathing, a groan, then a rustle of movement. But even as the tears cleared, her vision was still little more than a blur. *My glasses.*

Almost blind and struggling to breathe, she held the knife out and waved it from side to side. "Don't come any closer." The words rasped over Belle's raw throat.

"You stabbed me." Georgia's voice was close enough to make Belle jump. "You fucking stabbed me." There was incredulity in her words, but no trace of pain.

Belle used her left hand to roll the wheelchair backwards, trying to put distance between herself and the disembodied voice, and at the same time block the girl from coming around and grabbing her from behind.

The wheels hit something solid, stopping the chair with a jolt. Belle prayed it was the wall and used her left hand to fumble in her lap, hoping her glasses had fallen forward and were within reach. As she searched, Belle could hear Georgia moving around like a pacing tiger.

Chapter Nineteen

Her hair was the colour of champagne. When she moved, the light from the dusty windows picked out flecks of platinum. Arthur found himself lost in the way her pale head dipped as she stood before him.

"Professor Howell, I know my essay's due tomorrow, but..." Her hand, like an elegant bird, twisted the corner of the notebook she held close to her chest. "Well, this is difficult to talk about..."

Arthur leaned against the podium, shuffling papers that were already neatly piled. They'd had three similar conversations last semester; he knew where this was going. He wanted her to stop talking. He wanted her to walk out of his room. But more than anything, he wanted to feel her hair on his skin. He recalled the sensation: like silk, slippery and cool.

"Yes. Yes, I'm sure it is, but to keep giving you extensions..." He couldn't bring himself to look into her eyes for fear she'd see his desperation. "It's not fair on the other students, I..."

"Oh, no. Of course. I shouldn't have asked. It's just you're so kind and I'm..." Her voice like honey broke and with it his resolve.

He couldn't stop himself. He didn't try. His arms were around her and her head was against his shoulder. The other times, she'd come to him in his office. The first time had been innocent, her crying and him firmly seated on the other side of his desk. He'd handed her a box of tissues and watched with a galloping heartbeat as she plucked out a Kleenex between delicate fingers.

He could remember the moment when her visits stopped being innocent and became like a drug. She hadn't cried that time, but tears lined the rims of her dark blue eyes. She touched his hand, at first holding it then clutching it to her chest. He could feel the rise and fall of her breathing, the curve of her breast warm and firm beneath his hand.

He was forty-five, still a young man, but Christy was half his age. *Christy*. Her name tasted like silver on his tongue. Still holding his hand to her breast, she kissed him. Not on the lips, but the neck. Her mouth was warm and soft against his skin. Her breath sent a shudder through his limbs.

There were no windows in his office. No prying eyes to see him push her skirt up and kiss the flesh on her pale thigh as she moaned and cradled his head. Afterwards, he'd promised her anything – anything she wanted as she'd cried and talked about going to the Chancellor.

He loathed what he'd become, but like an addict, he couldn't stop. Each time she came to him, he'd *wanted* her to use him; he wanted to use *her* while hating her and himself. And yet even now, holding her in the lecture theatre, he wanted her.

"I don't want an extension." When she spoke, she turned her head so her breath caressed his neck. "I keep thinking about the things I let you do to me and…"

Arthur pulled back, but she clung to him. "Do to you?" His voice was shaking. "I only… I thought you wanted…" His mind was spinning. "Christy, please."

Her hand travelled up his spine. "I need to pass this unit, but with everything that's happened between us, I can't settle on my studies. You have to do this for me. You have to, Arthur." Her soft tone changed to something almost threatening.

He'd known all along, at least on some level that it would come to this. She didn't want him. She'd never wanted him. He was only a means to an end, a desperate middle-aged man reduced to a shuddering mess in her hands.

She was pulling away now, smiling. "I really care about you, Arthur, but I can't pass this unit without your help."

In that moment he saw her clearly. She was beautiful and sensual, her face and body clean and fresh. All the things he'd craved, but she was also hard and cold – manipulative. And worse than seeing her for what she truly was he saw himself through her eyes: pathetic, lascivious, and grubby, an old man pawing at her firm young body like a sex-starved animal.

He couldn't look at her, couldn't bear to see himself reflected in her eyes. "Get out." He choked out the words.

When she didn't move, he grabbed her arm and dragged her to the exit blinded by his tears and shame.

"Let go of me." Her voice more like broken glass than honey now, she shrieked and twisted in his grasp. Her blouse ripped and she stumbled forward.

"Arthur." Lynette Marshal, the assistant to the Head of English, stood in the doorway. "What's happened?" Her eyes shifted from Arthur's face to the girl now sobbing and clutching her blouse.

The memory so clear and painful melted into a haze of sound and voices. His left hand was numb; pins and needles jabbed at his skin. He tried to lift his head, but a shaft of pain snaked across his skull. Hangovers were often painful, but this was beyond any headache he'd ever experienced. Opening his eyes, the dazzling light made him wince and with the movement came nausea.

Arthur turned his head and a rush of liquid spewed over his lips, pooling on the floor beside his face. Images of Christy swarmed his fevered brain. The pain and longing felt fresh and raw as her features morphed into a different countenance, a kinder face, yet still as beautiful.

"Belle?" The word sounded hollow like a faint cry, spiralling out of a deep well.

As his vision cleared somewhat, Arthur recognised a ceiling above him, a circular light fitting, and the sounds of female voices. No stranger to waking on the floor and with dark spots in his memory, he tried to sit up. The movement caused a firestorm of pain in the back of his head.

The voices became clearer. Belle's usually warm tone sounded high and frightened. He didn't recognise the other voice, but the unmistakable anger added urgency to his need to move.

Groping for something to steady himself, he felt a tug on his wrists. The feeling was returning to his hands, but something was obstructing their movement. He yanked at the bindings and managed to pull free.

"You stabbed me. You fucking stabbed me." The words were clear even to Arthur's ringing ears. A woman was shrieking with disbelief and anger. Not Belle, but another woman.

Arthur sat up. Holding his head in his hands as though it might topple off his shoulders, he scrambled to his knees.

* * *

The room was used as a study. A desk sat beneath a crowded pin-board. To the right of it, bookshelves sagged under the weight of countless books and journals. But what drew Joan's attention was the items pinned to the board *and* the walls.

Pictures of Belle Hammer, at least thirty of them clipped from magazines and newspapers. Some printed on copy paper, all images of the author in various poses.

"What the heck?" Joan turned off the torch and slipped it into her pocket.

She took a step into the room and stood closer to the desk. Unlike the rest of the house, this space was messy and overcrowded. Judging by the worn office chair, the half-empty coffee mug, and the pair of slippers under the desk, this was where Arthur spent his time.

Joan tucked a lock of hair behind her ear. This room, like the rest of the property, told a story. But what Joan couldn't decide was if the story was tragic or threatening. Did it have anything to do with what she'd thought she'd noticed at Belle's house?

Reaching out a hand, she touched one of the photographs. Belle smiling, almost shyly, as she stood in a bookshop doorway. The walls around the shop were decorated with colourful graffiti art. The shot was most likely taken in a laneway in Melbourne or at least set up to look that way. It was the sort of picture that belonged on the back of a book jacket. Another image, obviously cut from a glossy magazine, showed Belle leaning against her car. Joan scratched her chin and looked down at the desk.

The author's books were stacked to the left of an aging computer. Looking over her shoulder, she noticed another set of the same books on the middle shelf of the bookcase. The spines were a different colour, but definitely the same novels.

She scratched her chin. Belle was a talented and beautiful woman. Joan could understand why men might be fascinated by her, but this was on a different level. The collection of pictures and books was bordering on obsession. The idea of Arthur Howell being obsessed with his neighbour was more than a little unsettling. But was he dangerous? What had Rena said about Arthur? Joan tutted, wishing she'd let the woman finish her gossipy tale.

She had no idea how or *if* any of what she was seeing mattered. As unlikely as it seemed, Arthur might just be a fan. Belle probably had thousands of fans that were just as obsessed as Arthur. And... he could have gone out with friends or called a taxi and gone into Mandurah. There were at least a dozen reasons why the man wasn't at home. *The front door was unlocked.* It was a small detail, but one that niggled at her reasoning.

Everything she'd seen that evening could have a reasonable explanation, but so many oddities surrounding one woman didn't sit right with Joan's rational mind. *Or my mind's not what it used to be.* There was no time to ponder the possibility of a dwindling mental capacity. She'd come looking for Guy's phone number. She'd gone as far as entering, if not breaking, so she might as well go ahead and search the study.

One thing she remembered from her conversation with Rena was that Arthur was a retired lecturer. There were very few personal items in the house, but plenty of books. Joan frowned and surveyed the shelves on the left wall. A man like Arthur valued the written word. If, like her, he was old-school about not trusting all his contacts to a mobile phone, he'd have an address book.

She nodded to herself and started with the desk drawers. Apart from a packet of envelopes, some push-pins, and an out-of-date coupon for ten percent off window awnings, the top drawer was empty. The second revealed nothing more interesting than a slip of stamps that were yellowed and peeling off the sticky backed paper.

Wondering if she'd misjudged not only Arthur's way of thinking but her own powers of deduction, Joan pulled open the bottom drawer and smiled.

"There you go, Roger." She slipped back into conversation with her deceased husband. "This is more like it."

But what she'd thought was an address book turned out to be more of a journal. Pages and pages of handwritten notes in large, tightly-packed cursive. Without her reading glasses, Joan held the book at arm's length to read Arthur's writing.

Squinting slightly, the words came into focus. Not a journal as such, but poetry. She was no expert, but the words and sentiments were sad and lovely at the same time. The sonnets expressed a gentle longing so at odds with her suspicions about Arthur being dangerous that a flush of shame crept up Joan's neck. Reading on, she found the feelings he articulated mirrored her own yearning in a way that was painful and mesmerising at the same time. Wanting to keep reading but having difficulty drawing breath, Joan closed the book and dropped it back into the drawer. She was the one in the wrong, reading Arthur's deepest thoughts and emotions, snooping around the man's house.

The air in the unheated house should have been freezing, but Joan felt suffocated. She left the study and closed the door, eager to escape the building and shrug off the feeling of dejection that seemed to cling to every wall and piece of furniture.

Once outside, she gulped in the cold, clean air and hurried down the porch steps. "Damn." The suddenness of her voice in the dark startled a roosting bird that fluttered up from a clump of trees. Without stopping she pulled open the car door and slid behind the wheel while the cantankerous bird shrieked out an angry litany.

"Now what?" She touched the keychain that dangled from the ignition. It was getting late. She should call it a night and go home. Hadn't she already gone above and beyond?

She turned the key and flicked on the headlights, noticing the way the beam washed any trace of colour from the ramshackle building. It occurred to her that Arthur might be on his way home and the easiest, most straightforward step would be to leave him a note.

She shook her head, annoyed that she hadn't had the idea sooner, then reached over to open the glovebox. "Probably easier than entering the poor man's house and going through his..."

The words dried up in her mouth. Joan's shoulders dropped and all thoughts of notes and Arthur Howell slipped from her mind. In the eighteen months since losing Roger, she must have opened the glovebox at least a handful of times. How was it possible that she'd never noticed the open packet of Larimax Throat Lozenges? *It's not possible.* But even as the familiar scent, both sweet and sharp filled the car, she still doubted her own eyes.

The smell of the lozenges was strong, almost too strong for an old packet. Joan reached out her hand and touched the package, half expecting it to vanish like the mist that surrounded the car. The packet, like everything in the car, felt icy. She held the lozenges up, turning the package under the interior light. Nothing supernatural about a half-eaten packet of lozenges. She gave a chuckle that was unconvincing and dry.

"If this is your idea of a sign…" She couldn't quite find the words to finish the sentence.

She held the lozenges close to her nose and closed her eyes, drinking in the familiar aroma of eucalyptus and honey. They were probably under the little pouch of tissues and the yellowing box of Band-Aids. Nothing mystical or otherworldly, just an old packet of throat lozenges jostled to the front of the glovebox on Arthur's bumpy driveway. But the world wasn't always that straightforward. She'd seen more than a few strange things over her sixty-four years. Not the least of them a healthy man dying in his sleep without making enough noise to wake his wife.

It didn't mean anything. She'd been reading too much into everything that had happened tonight. And what a crazy night it had been. She meant to put the lozenges back where she found them but couldn't bring herself to part with the little packet. Somehow holding the Larimax was like crossing time. Roger's hand would have held these throat lozenges, his fingers, like hers, around the packet.

Instead of putting the package back in the glovebox, Joan slipped it into her pocket. She flicked the headlights to high beam and put the car in reverse. Time for the craziness to end.

Chapter Twenty

Her hands closed around the frames. Belle grasped the spectacles with such urgency that she almost knocked them off her lap. Still holding the knife at arm's length, she somehow managed to get the frames in place. She thought she heard someone call her name, but when her vision returned all she saw was Georgia.

Unmoving, directly in front of Belle, stood Georgia. Her hands dangled in front of her body, palms out and coated with blood. The girl's expressionless eyes were fixed on Belle. Black smudges of mascara-lined her lower lids.

Belle's chest constricted, forcing her to breathe in short gasps. Her throat burned from where the carer had tried to choke her and the knife in her hand felt heavy, making her arm shudder under the weight.

"Please, just go. Just get out of my house." Her voice was an unrecognisable croak.

Georgia's expression remained blank as her head moved from side to side. The way she stood, her arms slack and splashed with blood, and her passive stare, reminded Belle of a TV show about zombies. Creatures with no soul that never stopped coming even if you stabbed or shot them. That's what the girl looked like, a soulless zombie.

When she spoke, her voice was flat and matter-of-fact. "I'm not leaving. There's no point. You took my life away." She took a step closer and Belle, using both hands now, waved the knife in front of her.

"All I've got is a crappy job at the care agency. The only good thing that came out of that was overhearing the director talking to your husband." She held her hands up and turned the palms in, staring at the blood. "Until I heard that call, I was almost ready to let it go. You were hurt." She shrugged. "That was enough until I heard Janice setting up a carer to come and look after you."

The girl was approaching, still shuffling, still zombie-like. Belle could see the bloody stain spreading from the girl's left shoulder, the dark patch blossoming on her uniform shirt.

Belle pulled one hand off the knife and tried to back up, but the wheelchair was against the far wall, leaving her nowhere to go. "So you *do* work for the agency." Belle wanted to keep her talking, but part of her, maybe the writer in her, needed to know how Georgia came to be in her home.

The girl nodded and a spark of interest flickered in her lifeless gaze. "Janice isn't very good at keeping things confidential. She couldn't wait to talk about our one and only celebrity client." As she spoke, Georgia rubbed her bloody palms on the front of her pants. "When she went on her lunch break, I snuck into her office. She'd jotted down the booking on a notepad." She gave a huff. "Stupid cow hadn't even bothered to put the details into the database."

"That's how you knew my address." Belle could see Georgia liked talking about how clever she was at figuring things out, so she tried to keep the conversation going. "That's how you knew I'd be expecting a caregiver. You knew I'd let you in the house."

Georgia nodded. She was more animated now, the swing between blank and excited was almost as frightening as the way the girl's gaze shifted between her bloody hands and Belle's face. It occurred to her that Georgia's mental state wasn't the result of the accident. No matter how much she'd lost when her dancing career ended, this level of mood swings and erratic behaviour stemmed from something deeper. Belle was starting to realise the girl had a serious mental illness.

"I knew you'd be alone. I met Lea a few times." Georgia took a step closer, seemingly oblivious to the knife Belle held. "She was okay, but sort of fat and sloppy. Bounding along on two good legs while I'm sitting behind the desk like a cripple." Her voice kicked up a notch. "That's not fair... I mean, I didn't plan on... on, you know."

Killing her? Belle wanted to scream the words, but instead remained silent. At least while Georgia was talking she wasn't attacking her. By playing for time, Belle might get a chance to get to the bathroom and lock herself in.

Belle didn't know if she should say something or just let Georgia tell it in her own way. Before she could decide, the girl was talking again, but now she was more animated, speaking in bursts like rapid gunfire. "I found a spot where I could pull off the road and hide my car. Then I pulled a fallen branch into the road." As she spoke, Georgia rubbed her fingers together and seemed to be enjoying the feeling of the blood on her skin. "I was taking a chance, but if someone else came along..." She jerked one shoulder. "They'd probably just move the branch and drive on."

The girl took a breath and blinked a few times, making Belle wonder if she was seeing the moment in her mind.

"When she got out of the car and started moving the branch, I stepped out of the bush. She recognised me and sort of smiled... I had the stick in my hand." She opened her right hand and gazed down at her bloody fingers. "I

148

didn't know what I was going to do, but she wouldn't shut up. She kept asking me questions. I had to make her be quiet and let me think. I had to get her in the car somehow."

Belle watched Georgia's movements and, as they became more jerky and sudden, she could almost see the terrible scene unfolding. The poor dead girl in the boot becoming more concerned, maybe even sensing danger, and Georgia exploding into violence. Belle's raw throat constricted and tears formed in her eyes. She could feel herself coming undone and almost wanting to give in to the emotional breakdown that was welling up inside her.

Georgia shook her head, her dark ponytail whipping around her face. "She was going to phone the agency. I had to do something, so I just… I pretended to cry and she tried to give me a hug." The words were tumbling out, heavy with panic. "When I got close to her..." She held up her left hand, circling an invisible body. "I pulled her in and... and…" A long sigh escaped the girl's mouth. "I rammed the stick into her neck."

Even though she knew this detail was coming, Belle had a hard time not gasping or crying out. She clasped her hand to her chest, pressing over the spot where her racing heart pounded under the skin.

For a moment neither woman spoke. With her heart still thumping, Belle managed to get her mind working again. "Can I have that drink now?"

Georgia, her arm still around an imaginary body, seemed lost in thought. For a moment Belle wasn't sure the girl heard her. Then like someone waking up, Georgia looked around then tipped her head back, seeming to stretch the muscles.

"Why not?" The caregiver moved to where the coffee table was standing askew.

Still holding the knife, Belle exhaled and let her hand rest on her knee. She wheeled forward, trying to position herself closer to the sofa.

The vodka bottle was on the rug, lying on its side. Georgia snatched it up and held it to the light. There was a little more than a quarter left. She pressed the lip to her mouth and swallowed.

"Here." Georgia turned, the movement sudden and jerky. Belle jumped and lifted the knife. "It's okay." The girl rolled her eyes, the smudged mascara giving her a crazed look. "I'm just giving you what you asked for."

Belle took the bottle in her left hand, never taking her eyes off Georgia's face. If she made another lunge, Belle intended to be ready. There were bloody prints on the glass, making the bottle slippery in her hand. She held the neck to her lips and even amidst all the violence and danger the smell made her shiver with craving. This would be her first drink in almost thirteen months.

She drank, taking only a small sip then grimacing at the bitter taste. To her surprise, rather than wanting to drain the bottle, her stomach cramped, forcing her to choke back the urge to gag.

Georgia was watching her with a pleased smirk lifting the corners of her mouth. Belle put the bottle in her lap and clamped it between her thighs. The moment struck her as bizarre. A few minutes earlier, Georgia was trying to choke the life out of her and now they were sharing a drink. She had to find a way to keep things calm until a chance of escape presented itself.

"You said you lost your foot a couple of years ago." She was taking a chance bringing up the accident, but maybe getting Georgia to talk would help dissipate the tension. *Or send her off the deep end.* "Do you remember the month?"

Georgia grabbed the plastic tub off the rug and dumped it on the coffee table. There were two mushed looking lamingtons stuck to the inside. "I remember the exact date."

Belle could hear a tremble in the girl's voice, but wasn't sure if it was anger or sorrow.

"It was the stupid Grand Final day." Georgia waved a hand in the air and slumped down onto the sofa. "That's what the party was about. This guy, I barely knew him but he always had plenty of grog and stuff, was a big fan of the Western Bulldogs." She looked into the cake tub and sniffed. "When his team won, he picked me up and stood me on the kitchen table. I didn't care about the footy, but it was nice having everyone staring at me and clapping, so I did a high kick and everyone cheered." She looked up. Her eyes were shiny. "My high kicks were amazing."

Belle wheeled forward, stopping at the arm of the sofa. Ahead was a direct run to the bedroom, but if she moved now she'd never make it before the girl was on her feet and after her. She needed a better head start and staring at the cake tub gave her an idea.

"So, yeah. I remember the date. The 1st of October 2016, the day I became a cripple." Georgia sounded tired, like all the anger and emotion had burned through her energy.

"Can I have a lamington?"

For a few seconds, the girl just stared at her puzzled.

"I haven't eaten since yesterday," Belle pushed on.

Georgia's brows drew down as she looked from Belle to the cake tub. Without answering, the girl leaned forward and grabbed a gooey looking cake. Keeping her eyes on Belle, she pushed the lamington into her mouth, devouring it in three bites.

Doing her best to look hungry, Belle bit her lip then rubbed her fingers across her mouth while watching Georgia eat. The act seemed to be working. The girl picked up the last cake and bit into it. Belle leaned forward counting each chew. *Four chews, swallow. Four chews, swallow.* When Georgia was done, she dragged her bloody hand across her face, leaving a smear of chocolate and blood. Torturing Belle seemed to bring her almost as much pleasure as the spongy coconut cakes.

While it was true that she was hungry, looking at the reddish brown streaks on the girl's face made Belle want to vomit. If she survived, she didn't think she could ever look at a lamington without feeling sick. It didn't take much acting skill to slump back in the wheelchair and look disgusted.

"You're so used to getting everything you want. I bet when you drove off and left me screaming for help, it never crossed your mind that I'd come looking for you." It seemed the sugar injection had reignited the girl's bitterness. She gave a scornful laugh and propped her feet on the coffee table, one hand clasped to her stomach. "If your husband wasn't on his way back, we could really stretch this out." She let her head fall against the back of the sofa. "Who knows? Maybe I'll hang around and meet him."

Belle's stomach rolled in a slow, sickening flip-flop. It hadn't occurred to her that Georgia would be insane enough to wait for Guy. But she'd seen enough to believe the girl was unhinged enough for anything. She clenched her fist around the knife, feeling the handle slip in her sweaty grasp. Guy was strong; he could take care of himself, but with the element of surprise and Georgia's unflinching approach to violence, anything was possible. Even as she worried over Guy's safety, something played at the edge of her thoughts. Something the girl had mentioned resonated in Belle's mind, but she couldn't quite make the connection.

And then, just as Belle hoped, Georgia stood and headed for the dining room. "I'm going upstairs." She jabbed a finger in Belle's direction. "Don't try anything because you won't get very far." That blank look was creeping over her face again. The lack of emotion in the girl's eyes made the hairs on the back of Belle's neck quiver.

When Georgia disappeared, Belle dropped her head and let out a shaky breath. She'd noticed how ravenously the girl ate *and* that she visited the upstairs bathroom after each meal. Going all that way just to urinate made no sense when Belle's ensuite bathroom was much closer. But it made perfect sense if Georgia was making herself vomit and wanted privacy.

With only minutes before the girl returned, Belle dumped the knife in her lap with the vodka bottle and headed for the bedroom. As she rounded the sofa, she came to a stop. Arthur was gone. The cords were there, heaped haphazardly on the rug, even the blue scarf that had been his gag; but the injured man had disappeared.

Belle looked around the room as though expecting him to appear. She had no idea how he'd managed to move while both she and Georgia were in the sitting room. But with time running out, Belle couldn't stop to search for him.

Pushing with all the force her shoulders could muster, she entered the bedroom. There was a sound on her blind side. Startled, Belle turned the chair ready to back up.

"Where is she?" Arthur sat slumped on the floor, his back to the wall just inside her bedroom.

Before she could answer, Georgia's footfalls echoed on the stairs. "Get up, Arthur." Belle leaned over, trying to get a grip on his arm. "We need to lock ourselves in the bathroom."

He took hold of the arm of her chair and tried to pull himself up, but his weight tipped the wheelchair and for one sickening second Belle felt herself falling. Arthur's face came close to hers. His eyes were frighteningly askew, one lid drooped, the other wide. He groaned and let go of the chair. The force dropped Belle back down and scooted the wheels forward.

"Go." He waved her forward while using the wall to brace himself half standing.

With blood whooshing in her ears, Belle hesitated. "Come on, we…" The plea died on her lips as Georgia appeared in the doorway.

Chapter Twenty-one

Guy leaned back and closed his eyes, willing his mind to relax. The seat was narrow, restricting his movements. The woman beside him slumbered in what sounded like a deep sleep with her elbow encroaching on his space. Economy class was the best the airline could offer at such short notice and he was grateful to be on his way back to Belle, although a small selfish part of him wished he'd waited for the next flight.

With the sound of the engine humming in his ears, the last conversation he'd had with his wife played over in his mind. When he told her the movie was a wash-out, she'd asked him when he'd be home. At the time he thought nothing of it, but after hanging up he started wondering why she hadn't asked for details. Normally, Belle would have wanted to know what had happened. He reached to rub his hand over his eyes and his elbow hit the window.

"Shit." He rubbed his arm while the woman beside him snored in her sleep and shifted a few centimetres further in his direction.

Belle was always the one who wanted to talk things out, always worried about his feelings, yet on the phone she sounded shrill and demanding and more worried about the girl from the care agency than his career. If he didn't know better, he'd be pissed. But the Belle he knew was never quick to anger and always put him first. Her attitude made no sense.

Giving up on sleep, he opened his eyes and stared into the vast blackness outside the window. He wasn't the world's most sensitive man, but his gut told him something was wrong. The sense of dread stewing in the pit of his stomach only increased when he tried to call his wife back and the call had gone to voicemail.

Turning the conversation over in his mind, he kept coming back to Katrina and her threats. Had she carried through on her promise to make his wife suffer? If Belle knew about his fling with Katrina, it would explain why their last conversation was so strained.

His only hope of pulling together their fractured relationship was to get home and come clean, to tell Belle the truth... or the part about Katrina. As for the rest... sometimes he wasn't sure what the rest was. The torture was not knowing. Not knowing what was waiting for him when he got home and not knowing if Belle could forgive him if she knew the things he'd done.

Guy checked his watch. The plane would land at five a.m. Perth time. By the time he made it through customs and drove home it would be close to seven o'clock. The aeroplane hit a pocket of air and the cabin dropped then shuddered. Apart from a few nervous yelps, the other passengers seemed docile, lost in their own thoughts and problems. He glanced at the woman beside him, envying her sound slumber.

The thought of jamming ear-buds in and watching a movie was even less appealing than listening to the woman's snores. With nothing but regrets to occupy his mind, Guy continued to watch the night sky slip past the window.

* * *

"Hey." Belle wasn't sure if Georgia was yelling at her or in surprise at seeing Arthur free and partially on his feet.

Not waiting to find out, Belle pushed towards the bathroom door. She was halfway across the room when the girl's hand fell on the back of the chair. "No you fucking don't." Georgia's voice was full of outrage.

The chair jerked back, the wheels spinning under Belle's fingers. She twisted in the seat, meaning to wrench the girl's finger off the handles and stab at them if necessary. But as Georgia's face loomed over her, Arthur appeared.

He stumbled towards the caregiver, arms up like a wounded bear, and fell on the girl. "Go, Belle." His voice was shaky, but loud.

As Georgia moved to free herself from his grasp, Arthur pulled her sideways. Belle wasn't sure if he had lost his balance or dragged the girl to the floor deliberately, but they both tumbled and their combined weight hit the hardwood with a thud.

Belle started to turn the chair, meaning to pull the girl off Arthur, but his body dropped lifelessly on top of Georgia. As the caregiver cursed and squirmed trying to get the man off her, Belle could see Arthur's hand lying slack on the floor.

"Arthur." Belle hesitated, but when his head lolled to the side, she saw his eyes were closed.

Georgia had almost freed herself from Arthur's weight when Belle spun the chair and headed for the bathroom. She could hear the girl's laboured breathing as she pushed through the doorway and rotated the wheels. Georgia was less than a metre away when Belle grabbed the door. For an instant her hand slipped on the wood and she almost lost her grip.

Crying out in frustration as much as from fear, Belle used her elbow to slam the bathroom door. As the knob moved, Belle clicked the lock. Arms shaking, she dumped the knife and vodka bottle on the tiles and pushed herself up on her good leg. Georgia hit the door with enough force to make the wood jump.

Belle let out a shriek and almost lost her balance, grabbing the side of her wheelchair to stop herself from falling. Wobbling, she grabbed the doorknob for stability and flicked on the light. Then, still on one foot, she reached up and slid the bolt in place.

"Open the door, Belle." Georgia's voice was low, almost a growl.

The knob jiggled then was still. Belle lowered herself back into the chair and backed away from the door. For the first time since the caregiver arrived, Belle felt a measure of control after what had become a nightmarish couple of days. Maybe it was that she felt a modicum of safety with a locked door between them. Or it could be that without the constant threat of violence, her mind was working more clearly?

She took her time, scanning the room. It was a large space for a bathroom. The luxury of the double shower at one end and a tub at the other was one of the things that had attracted Belle to the property in the first place. But all she cared about now was securing the door.

The chair's wheels squeaked over the tiles as she pulled up in front of the toilet. The removable toilet chair was light-weight and easy to lift. Belle leaned forward and hoisted the chair up, doing a quick balancing act with one hand as she backed up and spun around. Turning the chair's frame on its side, she wedged the arm under the doorknob. Then using her good leg, she knocked the leg in place.

Satisfied that the frame would hold, Belle spun around and turned on the tap. With no heating in the tiled space, the bathroom was one of the coldest rooms in the house. Despite the chill in the air and the icy shock, she splashed water on her face. Gasping, Belle cupped water in her hand and dumped it on the back of her neck. Before turning the tap off, she lowered her mouth to the jet and drank.

For the first time in days, she felt really awake. Awake and more like her old self. *I don't know who my old self is.* She'd spent so much of her adult life drunk or close to it, remembering who she really was didn't come easy. *All on your own?* No. She grabbed a towel off the rack and patted her face dry. That voice wanted to burrow into her brain but she refused to let it. She had more important things to worry about, things like Georgia's story about losing her foot.

Since the moment the girl accused her of the hit and run accident Belle had denied any involvement. And yet even as she tried to convince the girl she had nothing to do with the accident, a small voice inside her whispered otherwise. How many times had she driven when she knew she was over the legal limit? How many close calls had she had after a few too many glasses of wine? Was it possible that she'd hit the girl and didn't remember it? The doubts had squirmed in the back of her mind like a nest of snakes.

Belle stared down at the vodka bottle, then picked it up and sat it on the vanity unit beside the sink. Something Georgia said left Belle with no doubts. So distracted by the vodka, Belle had only taken in parts of the girl's story. But now in a quiet moment, a moment where the air felt charged with danger like the stillness in the eye of a storm, Belle recalled the girl's words. *The 1ˢᵗ of October 2016, the day I became a cripple.* It was also the day Belle's nephew, Jack, was born.

The memory that sprang to mind was a happy occasion, filled with frantic energy and joy. In light of what she now knew, the recollection reminded her of a glossy white stone streaked with pink quartz she'd once found half-buried in the earth: beautiful and perfect. Only when the stone was lifted it revealed a nest of bugs scurrying and squirming in the light.

Chapter Twenty-two

The ground under Joan's feet was swampy, sucking at her shoes like a wet mouth. No matter how hard she pulled, her feet wouldn't move. The lake rippled. Its water, an eerie pinkish orange, shifted under a light breeze. Fine mist hung over the water, rolling towards the shore.

Roger, dressed in his gardening clothes, stood knee deep in the strange pink water, arms hanging loosely at his side. His mouth moved and with it puffs of mist blew past his lips. His posture was relaxed, but the white puffs were chugging out of his mouth with urgency. He was trying to tell her something or call her towards him.

Joan reached out a hand, pleading with him to come closer, but her husband remained offshore and out of reach. A sense of misery, so heavy and dark, washed over her; tears stung her eyes. As she watched her husband continue his soundless entreaty, something grey and sleek flicked beneath the water.

"Roger." She screamed his name, trying to warn him about the thing now circling his legs.

Joan wrenched with all her strength and her left foot came unstuck. But as she moved closer to the water's edge,

Roger's eyes widened in horror and the water churned around him like frothy blood.

"Run, Roger." The words, jagged and tortured, tore out of her. But it was too late. With a splash from its razor-sharp fin, the grey monster dragged him beneath the foaming water. The mist swirled in the spot where her husband had stood, then settled into an undisturbed cloud.

Clawing at the sandy bank, Joan tried to reach the water. When she looked down, her hands were bloody, the nails ragged. She gave a hiccupping scream and woke in a bath of sweat.

Instinctively, she turned, looking for her husband's familiar shape, but saw only the undisturbed covers on Roger's side of the bed. Her heart racing, she reached up and flicked on the lamp. In the eighteen months since waking to find him dead, she had had many nightmares, but none as otherworldly and strange as the one she'd just experienced.

As she sat up and took a sip of water from the glass she kept on the nightstand, the details of the dream were already fading, leaving only a sense of impending danger and foreboding. She opened her mouth to speak, but summoning the image of her dead husband seemed less comforting on the heels of such a vivid nightmare. Instead, she checked the time on the clock on Roger's side of the bed, another relic of her life as one half of a pair. 4:49 a.m. The time was what her mother would have called an ungodly hour. Joan shivered, unsure if it was the early morning chill that shook her bones or the idea of an hour so dark and bleak God dared not exist in it.

Still unsettled and knowing sleep was out of the question, she threw back the covers. Intending to make a cup of strong tea and watch the sunrise, Joan pushed her feet into fuzzy blue slippers and grabbed the throw from the end of the bed, draping it around her shoulders as she scuffed through to the kitchen.

The sun was still at least an hour away from rising, but glancing through the kitchen window she noticed the night had taken on the flat grey quality that signalled morning. With the temperature dipping, Joan clicked on the bar heater and pulled the throw up on her shoulders and waited for the kettle to boil. There was a singular peacefulness that came with early rising. The silence of the bushland surrounding her house, an expectant hush just before the magpies cried out their morning song. The smell of cold morning air as the night disappeared into dawn.

As the kettle bubbled and clicked off, Joan was unaware of the joys of the morning. Hand poised over a washed-out looking china mug, her thoughts drifted to another kitchen: Arthur's. She'd only glanced at the empty room, but now another detail of the house plummeted into focus.

Joan dropped the teabag into the mug but didn't continue making the drink. "What was I thinking?" She spoke to the empty room, unable to believe she'd missed something so important.

Dressed in a dark fleecy tracksuit, she rushed into the bedroom and kicked off her slippers. Five minutes later, teeth brushed and wearing the same sleep-rumpled clothes, she pulled on her joggers and raced for the kitchen.

Stopping only long enough to turn off the heater and grab Roger's jacket and her car keys, she flew out of the back door and down the steps. The last time she'd left the house without running a comb through her hair was the morning the ambulance carried her husband away. Today, she moved with a great deal more of certainty.

Last night she'd let the discovery of an old packet of throat lozenges convince her that she was behaving like a mad woman. Now with the memory of Arthur's wallet sitting on his kitchen table, she thought otherwise.

"Who goes out and leaves their front door unlocked and their wallet at home?" She was talking to herself and not an imaginary image of her long-dead husband.

She'd awakened with a sense of dread. As she clunked the gearstick into reverse and edged down the winding driveway that feeling grew. She'd known from the moment she left Belle's house that something was wrong. Finding Arthur's strange study and his obsession with the author had muddied the waters; it had shaken her certainty. And then the throat lozenges in the glovebox…

Joan shook her head as the car bumped onto Silver Gum Lane. She wasn't as sure about the lozenges. Only that finding the packet in the car while sitting outside Arthur's ramshackle house – a house draped in a misty darkness – had knocked the wind out of her. But more than that, now the lozenges reminded her of how much faith Roger had placed in her opinion. If he were here, she knew he'd tell her to follow her instincts. Now that she had her second wind, she intended to make two stops. One to see if Arthur had returned home and the other, a stop she should have made last night. To talk to Belle Hammer.

* * *

For a while there was silence. At first, Belle kept her gaze trained on the bathroom door, but as the minutes stretched into an hour, her head nodded forward and for a while, she slept.

"Let me in." The whisper startled Belle awake. For a moment there was nothing but the sound of her own breathing. Then another whisper. "Let me in." The words were a hiss, low and vicious. Georgia's voice sent a ripple of fear up Belle's aching spine.

She backed the chair up until it was pressed against the vanity, putting about a metre between her and the door. Without a watch or phone, she had no way of knowing how long she'd been in the bathroom. The only indication of time was the grey light filtering in through the obscured glass window. It wasn't morning, but close.

Turning to reach the sink, Belle groaned at the burst of pain in her neck. She explored the area with her fingertips and winced at the soreness where the girl's fingers had pressed into the soft spot just above her sternum. The inside of her throat felt swollen and raw. Georgia had tried to kill her. If Belle hadn't stabbed at her with the knife, she might have succeeded.

Leaning over the sink, she turned on the tap and drank. The cold water worked like needles on her injured throat. Her empty stomach clenched and cramped at the shock, leaving Belle gasping. Then catching a glimpse of herself in the mirror, she let out a cry that was equal parts misery and disbelief.

The woman staring back at her was almost unrecognisable with her cropped, spiky hair, and a dirty bandage dangling from a bruised cheek. But most frightening was her eye. The white of it had transformed into a bloody orb that looked stark and gory against the blue of her iris. The overall look was that of a desperate and traumatised woman. *Is that what I am? Is that who I've become?*

Behind her, the door shuddered under the weight of another hammering, then more crashing followed by the twang of a door slamming somewhere in the house. Belle recognised the sound as the front door and a small glimmer of hope ignited in her chest. Maybe it had worked. Georgia had given up and was leaving. She pushed forward until her knees were against the bathroom door and turned her head to the side.

She listened, waiting to hear the sound of an engine. Fists clenched into tight balls, she willed the noise to start. And then it came, the hum of a car signalling the ordeal was over. But the sound morphed from a hum into a groan and Belle realised it was coming from her own throat. She croaked out a laugh even though there was nothing funny about the way her back ached from too many hours in the chair, and the little spark of hope that was turning into a thick clog of despair, constricting her breathing until she felt like her chest was on fire.

She leaned her head against the door as dry soundless sobs wracked her aching body. The idea of stumbling out of her chair and curling into a ball on the floor seemed more appealing than spending another minute hunched in the wheelchair.

She looked around and spotted the towel she'd used to dry her face. It wasn't much but it would be something to lie on. Belle turned the chair so she was facing the shower cubicle, then with the stiffness of an old woman she leaned down and threw the towel on the tiles. At the same moment, the window at the other end of the bathroom exploded inwards.

Glass pelted the floor, bathtub, and toilet. Instinctively, Belle ducked her head and curled her arms around her knees as shards landed like hailstones on the back of her neck and head. She felt something sharp hit the edge of her ear, and cried out.

Chapter Twenty-three

Arthur's house was as Joan had left it the night before: empty and desolate. After a quick trip through the sitting room, she picked up the black leather wallet from the two-seater kitchen table and flipped it open. Not meaning to snoop, Joan couldn't help staring at the man's driver's licence. In the photo Arthur looked younger, his skin tighter at the jawline and his hair short and cut rather stylishly. The renewal date told her the licence was almost five years old.

Joan snapped the wallet closed and put it back on the table. After a cursory glance around, she was satisfied the homeowner was nowhere to be found.

Back in the sitting room, Joan paused. "So..." She stretched out the word while gazing at the front door. "No money, no car, and the front door left unlocked." It didn't take a detective to guess the man had popped out, maybe for a walk. "A walk he didn't return from." If she'd been less consumed by the mystery, it would have occurred to her that talking to herself was becoming quite a habit.

Satisfied that she'd seen enough, Joan ran out of the house and hurried back to her car. The sun was rising, cool streaks of light bounced off her red Toyota, their rays not yet powerful enough to cut through the early morning mist. Hardly noticing the cold, she climbed in the car.

This time she didn't waste time reversing. Instead, she performed a sharp three-point-turn, hitting each point with jarring speed. There were only three properties on Silver Gum Lane. After that their closest neighbour was an eight-minute drive away. It seemed unlikely that Arthur would set out on a twelve-kilometre walk to visit Edward and Rowena Bathright, a retired couple who spent a good deal of the year prospecting. Not that Joan kept tabs on everyone in Lake Stanmore, but she did remember Rowena mentioning spending July in the Goldfields somewhere near the edge of the Nullarbor Plain.

Discounting a walking visit to their closest neighbours and, in light of Arthur's obsession with the author, Joan felt certain that whatever was going on at the Hammers', Arthur was involved. It was a certainty so powerful that she tore out of Arthur's driveway, kicking up a spray of pea gravel.

Rounding the bend, Joan snatched a glimpse at the time display. 5:26 a.m. Almost a reasonable hour to turn up asking questions. When her gaze returned to the road, the changing light momentarily took her by surprise, making a shadow appear to jump forward. Without thinking she veered left, breaking and turning the wheel at the same time.

For a split second, the small car swung sideways. The wheels locked with an ear-piercing squeal. Joan released the brake, but it was too late to stop the Toyota from spinning off the road and across the gravel shoulder. Back on the brake, her hands gripped and pulled as she fought to control the wheel. A dry popping sound filled the spinning car and Joan let out a scream of pain and surprise.

With the cry still bouncing off the car's windows, the Toyota came to a jerking halt, its bonnet connecting with the trunk of a gum tree. The impact was little more than a ping, but the blow shook a dry branch loose, sending it plummeting onto the roof of the vehicle. The limb landed with a violent *whack* and bowed the roof.

* * *

Belle raised her head as the last fragments of glass *tinged* on the bathroom floor. On the other side of the window, Georgia used one of Belle's crutches to punch out the remaining shards from the frame. Her lips were bunched together with grim determination. Clumps of hair pulled loose from her ponytail and flicked around her shiny face.

As the girl climbed over the sill, glass crunched under her hands and feet, but she seemed unaware of the razor-sharp fragments. Belle grabbed at the toilet seat, trying to pull if free from the door and escape. Behind her, Georgia landed in the bathroom with a grunt. Her right leg tipped at the knee and she stumbled. She regained her balance by grabbing the edge of the vanity, while her unwavering gaze somehow remained detached and focused at the same time. She pounced forward and grabbed the back of the wheelchair.

Belle scrambled for the vanity where she had left the knife, but before her fingers could close on it the girl swiped it out of reach, sending it clinking into the sink. "Georgia!" Belle held up an arm, shielding her face in case of a blow. "Please, whatever you're thinking of doing, it's not too late to stop."

The girl held Belle's gaze with pupils that almost eclipsed her irises, but didn't speak. Then leaning over Belle but not touching her, she wrenched the toilet frame out from under the doorknob. As she moved around the wheelchair and unlocked the bathroom door, Belle glanced at the window. Without the frosted glass, she could see the trees were tinted silver in the first rays of light. It occurred to her that this might be the last time she saw the sunrise. A new crop of tears filled her eyes.

With the door open, Georgia turned and grabbed the wheelchair. She didn't speak as she pushed Belle past Arthur's unmoving form and through the sitting room.

"Please," Belle tried again. "I know what you think of me, but let me explain."

Georgia stopped next to the sofa. "I'm not interested in what you've got to say." She bent and grabbed the cord she'd used to bind Arthur. As she did, the sleeve of her shirt rode up and Belle caught a glimpse of the skin beneath. Gashes striped her wrists. Some were crusty with blood and some were white scars. The same marks could be seen all the way up to her forearm.

The girl saw Belle staring and snatched the sleeve down.

"I know you didn't mean to kill Lea. I'll help you explain what happened to the police. I can…" Belle tried to come up with something that would give Georgia hope, but judging by the impassive look on the girl's face she wasn't doing very well.

As well as disappearing upstairs to vomit and hurt herself, and judging by the girl's pupils and the way she seemed oblivious to the pain from her still-bleeding shoulder, Belle guessed the girl was taking something. Maybe not meth, but something chemical was fuelling her rage. Either that or Georgia was completely insane. No, Belle corrected herself, the girl's behaviour was bordering on maniacal.

Georgia ignored Belle's pleas and flung the cord over her. Belle twisted and grabbed the cable, trying to pull it out of the girl's hands.

"Hey." Lacing her fingers at the back of Belle's head, Georgia snatched a handful of hair and twisted. "Stop it." She gave Belle's head a painful shake.

Belle gasped as Georgia's strong grip lifted her scalp, but she continued to struggle. The idea of being bound cut through the fear and cancelled out the idea of reasoning with the girl. If she let Georgia tie her to the chair, she'd be completely helpless just like … Just like she'd been in the back of that man's car. The weight of that realisation hit her like a mallet. The memories weren't something she'd seen in a movie or brought on by stress. Instead of slowing her down, the clarity of that gut-wrenching assault ignited something inside her – something she'd been pushing down since she was four years old. Rage.

Belle reached around and grabbed the girl's hand, pulling at her fingers until she managed to loosen one. She gave the digit a violent twist and the girl's grip slipped. Belle pulled her head free and turned in the chair. She registered Georgia's look of surprise and used the girl's momentary pause to her advantage. It might be a losing battle, but Belle intended to fight for survival even if it meant having every hair on her head ripped out. Belle pulled her fist back and landed a punch on the bloody spot on the carer's shirt. Because she was sitting, Belle had to strike upwards, and the blow didn't land with as much force as she'd hoped. Still, Belle felt the wound beneath the girl's shirt squelch and the caregiver barked out a shocked cry.

The punch didn't slow Georgia down. She lunged for Belle's head again, her nails raking Belle's ears, tearing open the wound made by the flying glass. As Georgia's fingers ripped at Belle's skin, her glasses jerked sideways almost becoming dislodged.

The threat of losing her ability to see forced Belle to stop struggling long enough to clamp her spectacles in place. This seemed to be the opportunity the girl was waiting for. She zagged right and brought her fist down on Belle's injured knee.

The impact seared through every nerve in Belle's body. The pain was electric and resounded in waves that cut out all thought. Arching back in the chair, she let out a scream that came from deep in her chest; a sound that drained her body and left her slumped and moaning. The rage that had

169

burned so hot only moments ago died as quickly as it had ignited, leaving her spent and gasping for breath.

Vaguely aware of the movement around her, Belle felt something slide over her shoulders and pull in at her waist. Still sucking in each breath around the waves of agony spiralling out from her knee, Belle became conscious of the cord pinning her arms to the wheelchair.

Georgia wound the cable around Belle's body a second time, pulling the restraint tight around her stomach and fastening it at the back of the chair.

"No." It was the only coherent word Belle could muster while twisting and wrenching at the cord.

"I can't do this anymore." Georgia was pushing the chair now, talking and moving with speed. "It's got to end. It hurts too much. It'll be better when it's all done."

Belle tried to make sense of what the girl was saying, but her words seemed disjointed and jumbled. With each jostle and bump of the chair, Belle's kneecap felt like it was ripping at her flesh and tendons. They were moving through the dining room and heading for the back door. At some point Belle was vaguely aware of one of her slippers sliding off and falling away.

When they emerged onto the deck, the cold air slapped at Belle's cheeks, pulling her attention away from the pain and towards the cold blue sky. The misty vapour in the air reflected reddish sparks across the firmament. The colours and the smell reignited something in her mind, a need to keep fighting, a stubborn determination to overcome helplessness and survive.

"This will help. It will help us. It'll make it better." Georgia's voice rose and fell in a one-sided conversation that made little to no sense. All the while she pushed the chair onwards with a sort of marching resolution that told Belle they were nearing the end of the ordeal. There would be no more games. No more chances to escape.

Georgia steered towards the ramp and the pool came into view and with it the girl's intention became clear. Belle bucked under her restraints, snaking her wrists and pulling back and forth as panic sent her brain into overdrive.

"It'll all stop. I can... I can make it stop." Georgia continued talking, her voice echoing off the water as they drew closer to the pool.

Chapter Twenty-four

The engine was still running, the noise gravelly like a chain-smoker's cough. Raising her left hand made her arm shake. Her entire body was trembling, but the sight of her pinkie finger bent to the side at an almost perfect ninety-degree angle made her stomach flip and swirl.

Above Joan, the car's roof dipped dangerously close to her head. She swallowed back an acidy taste that washed over her tongue, then turned off the engine. Blinking and unsteady, she used her right hand to open the door. With each movement she paused, waiting for a stab of pain from the discovery of a new injury, but it seemed the broken finger was the only damage. That and her sudden inability to stop shaking.

Placing her feet on the soggy ground helped; it pulled the situation from surreal into something close to manageable. An accident, a relatively small one. Not a catastrophe, not even close. Joan leaned on the open door and surveyed the damage. The odour of engine oil, thick and sweet, permeated the air. The roof was dented and the front of the car looked a mess, but it could have been worse.

She held her left hand to her chest surprised that her injured finger felt so numb. *It looks bloody gruesome.* Another stomach flip told her it was best to avoid staring at the ghastly digit. With every passing second, her heart rate was decreasing. Another few deep gulps and she was able to catch her breath.

The road was less than a few metres away, but deserted and likely to remain so. This was the first car accident Joan had been involved in, barring a few scrapes when reverse parking at the shopping centre. As her pulse settled, her mind began to work through the best way to proceed. The vehicle would have to be towed to the nearest garage. Thankfully her roadside assistance insurance would cover the costs. Using her uninjured hand, she reached into her pocket. Her fingers landed on the throat lozenges, but came up empty on the phone.

Still shaken from the crash, she reached around and dug into the other pocket. With a growing sense of alarm, she found nothing but a crumpled Kleenex. She'd left the house still dazed from the nightmare and in a hurry. Vaguely, she remembered pulling on her trainers, grabbing Roger's jacket and her car keys, but after that things got foggy.

"Damn it." She had been so absorbed with Arthur and Belle, she had raced out of the house, and not bothered to take the usual precaution of making sure she had her phone. *What was I thinking?* Thinking too much was what had got her into this predicament. *It was blood on the back of that car, I know it was.* Thinking too much was how she'd convinced herself that the residents of Silver Gum Lane were caught up in the middle of some sort of dangerous drama. And now, the drama was all hers.

The numbness in her hand was wearing off and her pinkie was starting to hurt. It more than hurt. It felt like the first joint was being squeezed by a pair of invisible pliers. Without her phone she had only two options: walk home and call a tow truck or go on to the Hammers' house and ask to use their phone. The first option meant a long walk in the cold, clutching her broken finger. Belle's place was just around the bend. As much as she didn't want to acknowledge it, a small part of her was glad of an excuse to knock on the Hammers' door.

Joan grimaced at her own deviousness. *Am I really going to use the accident as an excuse to find out what's happening in Belle's house?* She glanced down at her twisted digit and winced. She decided that was exactly what she was going to do. Without further consideration, she started back to the road.

* * *

Mist curled up from the water in lazy wisps. Belle could feel a breeze lifting her hair and chilling her skin. Georgia turned the wheelchair, bringing it to an abrupt stop near the pool's edge.

The girl crouched between Belle and the water, bringing their faces level. "I was going to kill myself." Her eyes were shiny, bouncing between the pool and Belle's face. "That was the plan. I'd come here and make you understand what you took from me then kill myself." Her teeth were chattering, making her words sound tremulous. "I didn't want to hurt that girl." She rubbed a hand across her forehead.

Despite the fear, Belle felt a pull of pity for the young woman who'd tortured and bullied her. "I believe you, but don't do this."

There were tears in Georgia's eyes, hanging unshed on her lower lids. She turned and looked at the pool. "Please, Georgia, killing me won't make anything better. It won't change what happened to you." Belle twisted her wrist, still trying to pull free of the cord. "I know how it feels to have something terrible done to you. I know what it's like to be helpless, but you don't have to ruin your life to make the pain go away."

She felt the cord give and turned her hand sideways, flattening it against the arm of the chair. She was playing for time again, but the things she was saying were true. She really did understand the rage and pain that came from being a victim.

"There are things worth living for. You just have to find them."

Georgia sniffed. When she turned back from the water, the tears were gone. "I have, Belle. I've found a reason to keep living." She leaned closer so their noses were almost touching. "I want to live knowing your life is over."

Belle shook her head. Nothing she said made any difference. She could see by the cold and faraway look in the girl's eyes that Georgia was unreachable. As Georgia stood and took hold of the wheelchair, Belle wrenched her hand back and it slipped out from under the cord.

The chair moved forward and suddenly. Belle's feet were at the edge of the pool.

She was past panic. Sheer terror drove her to scream. "Georgia, don't!" Her pulse was jumping, the blood thundering in her ears, making it almost impossible to focus while alarm bells screamed in her brain.

She wanted to jump out of the chair, even plunge into the water and try to swim, but with one arm still bound, the chair would drag her down. Desperate, she used her right ankle to flip back the footrest and planted her bare foot on the rough edge of the pool, hoping she could summon enough force to push back against Georgia's force. But as the chair edged forward, all Belle managed to do was slow the inevitable. With a grunt, the girl shoved the wheelchair forward and the ground disappeared from underneath Belle's foot.

Chapter Twenty-five

Joan rounded the bend and the Hammers' place came into view. The sun was almost up now. Pale light dappled the roof and the red pea gravel driveway, giving the house a cosy almost idyllic look. She held her injured hand close to her body and started up the driveway.

A few paces closer and Joan heard birds twittering in the trees to the right of the building. As she turned her head in the direction of the birdsong, another sound ripped through the air. A scream, agonised and piercing, set off a flurry of screeching from a flock of startled wattle birds that burst from the trees and took flight.

Joan clasped her right hand around her injured finger and jogged towards the house. As she neared the white car, her foot landed on a large stone and her ankle wobbled. The sudden shift in balance sent her stumbling forward onto one knee. She cried out and held up her broken finger, grateful that she was able to stop herself before her body hit the ground.

Without pausing to examine her knee, she was up and running while overhead a cloud of birds squawked and swirled. She reached the car, but didn't stop to inspect the smudge of blood. Instead, Joan ran to the front door and balling her good hand into a fist, she pounded on the same spot she'd knocked only the night before.

There was no sound from inside the house. Waiting less than a couple of seconds, she banged the door a second time. "Belle? Belle, it's Joan." She wasn't quite sure why she was yelling only that she wanted the author to know she wasn't alone.

She tried the knob and found the door locked. It couldn't have been more than thirty seconds since she heard the scream, not long but enough time for anything to happen. Banging on the door and shouting was getting her nowhere. With the memory of the scream still resonating in her ears, Joan stepped off the small porch and went in search of another way in.

Skirting the car, she made her way around the right side of the house, following a path of half metre slabs that led past the garage and between a thick crop of shrubs. The track darted alongside the house, tapering off at a wide area that housed a large green wheelie bin. A few metres further and she came to a window.

Shards of glass edged the sill below a gaping hole. Without touching the frame, she leaned her head in and surveyed the tiled floor and large bathroom. Joan tried to swallow but her mouth was dry. This room with its broken glass and tipped over furniture was the scene of something intense, something violent. Any doubts she had about what she'd seen the night before evaporated like the saliva in her mouth.

She glanced back at the narrow pathway and for a second she considered fleeing. Running back to her safe little house and calling the police. Even as her mind threw up reasons to go, Joan knew she couldn't turn her back on whoever had screamed.

Still cradling her broken finger, she pulled her good hand inside the roomy sleeve of Roger's jacket and grasped the window frame. As she stepped up onto the window, splinters of glass crunched under her trainers.

"This is crazy." Her voice sounded small and echoed as she dangled one foot inside the bathroom.

She wasn't a Hollywood action hero, just an aging ex-medical receptionist with a broken finger. Yet, here she was jumping through a broken window, coming to the rescue like a super-hero. *More like stumbling than jumping.* What, she wondered, would Roger make of all this. The string of thoughts was fleeting. As both her feet landed on broken glass, her gaze came to rest on the knife in the sink.

Stepping carefully across the floor, she picked her way to the open door where she paused and listened. The house was silent, no sound of voices or struggling. Breathing heavily now, she slipped through the bathroom doorway.

A breath caught in her throat. The destruction in this area was worse than the bathroom. A broken lamp tossed on the floor, drawers pulled loose from the dresser, their contents spilled and heaped on the bed, and photo frames smashed against the far wall. Joan had the sense she was following the path of a cyclone more than that of a human being.

Without thinking, her hand slipped into her pocket and clenched the packet of throat lozenges. She was out of her depth. Whatever was happening in the Hammers' house was beyond anything she'd imagined. The best she could do for Belle was to find a phone and call the police.

It was difficult to tell if a phone hid somewhere amongst the debris, so she crept further into the room intent on checking the bedside table. With any luck, she could call for help and then exit the building the way she'd entered. *What about the scream?* Could she really ignore what she'd heard and stand on the driveway like a coward waiting for someone else to act? Was that what old age did, make you weak with fear?

Her fingers crinkled the lolly packet and she felt a surge of defiance. No. Joan decided she wouldn't run like a terrified old woman. She'd find the phone, summon help, and then do what she could to help Belle. As Joan rounded the bed, she noticed what at first looked like more destruction: a pile of clothes heaped on the rug. Stepping closer, her heart jack-knifed and she realised it was a body.

"Dear, God." All thoughts of stealth vanished as she sunk to her knees next to Arthur's head.

She touched his face and was relieved to feel its warmth. Moving her fingers down, she pressed his neck. With her own pulse racing, it was difficult to focus all her senses on the tips of her fingers. For a moment there was nothing, but then she found the thready bump of his pulse. He was alive.

"Arthur." She leaned close to his ear. "Arthur, can you hear me?" Following her first aid training, she touched his hand. "Move your fingers if you can hear me." Movement, but not much. Only a twitch of his fingers, but a definite response.

She noticed a laceration and swelling on his forehead. "I'm going to roll you on your side." The manoeuvre was awkward; Arthur a dead weight and Joan only using one hand. As his head rolled, she spotted blood on the back of his head, sticky and matted in his grey hair.

As she settled the man's hand across his chest, it occurred to Joan that he might have been the one who smashed up the bedroom. After what she'd seen at his house, she had no idea what Arthur Howell was capable of *or* why he was unconscious in Belle's bedroom.

Standing was a monumental effort. Adrenalin, some left over from the car accident and then fuelled by the shock of finding Arthur, set her legs quivering. For now, Arthur's involvement didn't really matter. Getting the injured man medical help was a priority, but so was finding Belle and her carer. But wasn't it the vulpine look in the caregiver's eyes that had first set Joan's senses on edge? Her thoughts were spinning.

As she exited the bedroom, Joan clenched her teeth, preparing herself for what she might find. When she found the sitting room empty she felt a moment of relief, but that feeling was swiftly swallowed by dread. If the two women weren't in the sitting room, then where? Had Arthur done something to them?

She knew there were people who no longer bothered having a landline in their homes, and as she scanned the sitting room it became clear that the Hammers were like that. She should have checked Arthur's pocket for a phone. Cursing herself for not being on the ball, Joan spotted something that shut down all thoughts of landlines and mobiles. A woman's slipper, pink and shiny, lying on the floor just past an archway that looked like it led to the rear of the house.

Trance-like, she walked towards the slipper. The mundane item out of place in the dining area seemed somehow sinister. Glancing right, she spotted a doorway and the staircase. On the left, the kitchen and the back door. The last time she'd seen Belle, the woman was in a wheelchair so Joan quickly discounted searching upstairs.

The doorway next to the stairs was the obvious choice, but Joan hesitated. In that heartbeat of indecision, a small sound changed her course. One word faint but clear. *"Don't."* Panicked and clearly female, the voice came from outside.

Joan raced for the back door and tore it open. The cold wind blew back her hair as she looked left then right, searching for the source of the cry. The angle of the deck blocked much of the garden. It was only when she dashed forward that Joan saw the ramp and the two women at the edge of the pool.

Belle in the wheelchair, shaking her head and struggling, behind her the caregiver gripped the chair's handles. They were close to the water – too close. Joan opened her mouth to call out to the women, but before the words were out the unthinkable happened. The girl shoved the chair over the edge and into the pool. In the second when the wheelchair tipped, Belle reached up and grabbed the girl, pulling the girl into the water with her.

Joan saw them disappear. She heard the splash, sudden and shocking in the misty morning air. And still, her brain couldn't quite comprehend what was happening. A second slipped by, then two before she blinked and burst into action.

"Oh, God." Joan ripped off Roger's jacket and tossed it flapping in her wake.

She burst down the ramp, thumping the wooden boards with speed she didn't know her sixty-four-year old legs possessed. As she reached the paved area alongside the pool, Joan hopped on one foot and pulled off her trainer, dropping it with a dull thud. The second shoe took more effort and for one maddening second, she almost fell forward.

When she reached the edge of the pool her breath was already laboured, her heart hammering into her throat. Joan curled her toes over the rim and took two deep breaths.

Chapter Twenty-six

Icy water smacked the breath out of her lungs. As the chair sank, it tipped sideways in a blind flurry of bubbles and thrashing limbs before clunking down on the floor of the pool. Belle gripped Georgia's shirt, her fingers seizing on the fabric as the water obscured everything but her sense of desperation.

Something batted at her head as the chair settled at the bottom of the pool. Underwater, sound receded into a hollow muffle of air bubbles and swooshing as the two women struggled. Belle's glasses were gone, but close up she could see the girl's mouth open and her eyes wide with panic. The air in Belle's lungs was running out and the urge to open her mouth and suck in water was almost more than she could bear.

Georgia's fingers pushed at Belle's face like frantic eels digging at her skin. Belle released her grip on the girl and tried to push upward, but the cord still around her waist and left hand held her bound to her chair. Barely aware of the girl, the cold numbing of her limbs and the burning need for oxygen, Belle closed her eyes.

There's air in my lungs, enough to make it to the end of the pool. It was the mantra she used on her daily swims, the trick she employed to push past her own limits and swim underwater from one end of the pool to the other. *There's air in my lungs, enough to make it to the end of the pool.* On the second time, a familiar calm settled over her and Belle twisted her left hand sideways and out from under the cord.

With two arms free, she pushed down on the cord and wrenched her body sideways. The bindings loosened and her torso slid free. Digging at the water, she headed up only to be snapped back as the cord caught on her nylon leg cast.

The last precious bubbles of air burst from Belle's lips as she clawed at her leg and tried to pull upwards. With her lungs burning, her body took over and all conscious thought vanished in a frenzy of flailing limbs. Her mind was almost as numb as her fingers as her body reached its breaking point and shifted into a state of nearing semi-consciousness. Flashes like snapshots blinked in her brain. The beach at sunset. Her sister in her wedding dress. Foxy, the Jack Russell Terrier she'd had growing up. Red trainers with gold ribbon.

Belle's eyes burst open as a hand slipped under her armpit. A surge of energy like nothing she'd experienced before and she was moving towards the light. Then an explosion of sound and air.

"I've got you." The world was a blur of exquisite light and delicious air. "Come… Come on…" Someone, a woman was trying to speak, panting and talking. A strong hand held her around the chest, gripping her chin.

She almost recognised the voice, but her vision was unclear and her brain was still jittering between panic and relief. As she moved through the water aided by the unknown rescuer, her instincts took over and she began paddling her arms and kicking her good leg.

When her fingertips touched the ledge, Belle grabbed on, too weak to do anything but cling. Her rescuer let go of her armpit, and with a thunderous splash, Belle was left hanging on by her trembling hands.

Looking up, the light added to her inability to see. A figure, outlined by the sun, leaned over her. "Help me." The words were strained as the woman reached down and wrapped an arm around Belle's back.

Teeth chattering, her exit from the freezing water was somewhere between a bounce and a drag. With her chest and arms on the edge of the pool, the woman hauled Belle out of the water. When her legs rolled onto the paving, they were too numb for her to feel any pain.

For a while she lay motionless, panting. Her wet clothes clinging to her like frozen weights. Too cold and too numb to process what had just happened, Belle wanted only to be warm again.

"Oh, dear God." The woman spoke, but her words were only registering as sound. "Belle, where's your phone?"

Belle recognised her name and then the voice, familiar, almost comforting, even shaking, and clearly frightened cut through the fog. She tried to raise her head, but her body spasmed with chills.

"Sh…she too…took it." Belle's lips were moving, the words stuttering out. Her vision was clearer now, but not great.

She saw the woman's outline and heard her dripping clothes as she moved across the paving. "Don't…" Belle managed to raise her head. "Don't leave me… I can't see without my… without my glasses." The last two words were little more than a squeak.

A hand, damp but warm touched her face. "It's all right, dear. They're here." Her spectacles bumped over her nose and slid in place.

The woman's face came into focus. "Joan." For some reason, her elderly neighbour's face brought a fresh swell of emotion. Belle's lip trembled and without warning she was weeping.

Joan, on her knees beside Belle, took her hands and covered them with hers. She winced as though in pain. "It's all right, Belle." Her teeth were chattering, but her voice was calm. "I'm not leaving you. I have to get us blankets or we'll freeze to death. I'll be right back." She nodded, her wet hair flicking water in all directions. "Don't move. Just lie still until I come back." She spoke softly as though to a child. Then she did something that cut through the shock and made Belle listen and understand. Joan leaned over and kissed Belle on the forehead. The spot where the elderly woman's lips touched her skin was the only point of heat on Belle's body.

Belle gave her head a shake and reluctantly let go of Joan's hand. She watched the woman run barefoot up the ramp, her damp clothes clinging to her tall frame.

Once alone, Belle let her head rest on the ground and curled her fist against her chest. Realisation of what just happened was starting to dawn and with it a sense of hope. She'd survived. She was still alive and Georgia... A moment ago, Belle didn't think it was possible to be any colder, but now the chill seeped into her bones. Suddenly she felt small and vulnerable. As she used her shuddering hands to push up into a sitting position, she whimpered.

Georgia was in the water. Belle's brain reacted and she let out a half scream, croaky and dry on her lips. Instinctively, she planted her hands and shuffled back, trying to crab-walk away from the girl. Suddenly she was confused, surprised at Joan. *How could she leave me with her?*

But Georgia was no longer a threat. Surrounded by mist, her body floated face-down, her hair fanning out like dark tendrils. The girl's arms were splayed as her lower body hung beneath the water. Belle's arms buckled and her butt hit the paving. Things were clicking into place in rapid succession. The clunk as the chair hit the floor of the pool, Georgia's face panicked and frantic under the water. Joan's shocked voice asking for a phone. It really was over.

185

The backdoor thumped open and Joan was jogging down the ramp, arms overflowing with towels and blankets. Watching her neighbour approaching, Belle felt a tug of emotion for the woman who had saved her life only moments ago and was now endeavouring to give her whatever aid she could find.

She glanced back at Georgia's body, but Belle's own depleted body wasn't capable of feeling anything but relief. Relief she was alive *and* that the danger had passed.

"Here." Joan wrapped a blanket around Belle's shoulders, the sudden warmth felt like a minor miracle after the searing cold. "I found two phones upstairs. One was locked but the other was okay. I've called the police. I opened the front door so they can get in." As she spoke, Joan sat down and piled another blanket over Belle's legs.

As Joan smoothed the rug over Belle's knees, Belle noticed one of Joan's fingers. "You're hurt." She thought she had no emotion left in her, but the sight of the elderly woman's twisted finger set off a wave of misery. "I'm so sorry. Did I do that to you when you were pulling me out of the water?"

Joan held the hand up as if surprised to see the injury. "Oh, that." She tutted. "That wasn't you, dear. I had a minor accident on the drive over." There was a stoicism in her voice that reminded Belle of a nurse in an old war movie. The image was endearing and awe-inspiring at the same time.

Belle shivered. "Thank you. You saved my life." She picked up a towel from the pile Joan had plopped down on the paving. "You're freezing." She let her own blanket fall as she draped the towel around Joan's shoulder.

Joan accepted the towel and clutched it at her throat. "I only wish I'd got here sooner." She nodded to where Georgia's body floated in the water.

Belle leaned closer to her neighbour. "You're here now."

* * *

Guy gave up trying to call Belle an hour previously, but that didn't stop him glancing at his phone every few minutes. The endless hours of travel had been filled, not with regrets about the movie and his missed opportunity, but with a growing certainty that he'd blown the one thing in his life that really mattered: his marriage to Belle.

He swung the car onto Silver Gum Lane with a knot twisting in his gut. The silent treatment was never Belle's style. She knew. It was the only explanation for why she wasn't answering his calls. Katrina had made good on her promise and now Belle was suffering and so was he. But his pain didn't matter. All he could think about was how much pain this was causing his wife.

The road was quiet, the winter sun clearing the mist and warming the car as it raced past Arthur's driveway. For a second Guy slowed his progress. Belle's silence was something that could be explained, but Arthur too? It wasn't like the old guy to drop off the edge of the world like this, not when he'd promised to keep an eye on the place.

Guy knew his wife didn't like Arthur, but Guy enjoyed the old man's company. He was smart. He knew about books and plays. Stuff Guy had no idea about. He could be himself around Arthur, relax and just be. It seemed everyone in his life was competing with him in some way. In looks, talent, even in who they knew. But not Arthur.

Guy pushed his sunglasses up on his head and rubbed his eyes. He couldn't remember when he'd last slept, not on the plane that was for sure. Telling himself that Arthur was probably flat out somewhere sleeping one off, Guy coasted into the bend. His eyes felt so puffy and stiff that he almost missed the glint of light off the rear end of the car, only catching sight of it at the last minute.

Tyres screeching, he juddered to a stop. For one gut-wrenching moment, he thought it was Belle's car but now, standing still, it was clearly a different vehicle.

"What the fuck?" Guy looked back the way he came as though an explanation could be found on the empty road. There was no reason for another car to be this close to his house. His thoughts stuttered. Unless it was Katrina. "Jesus."

He turned off the engine and jumped out, his chest constricting as he approached the car. On closer inspection, the damage wasn't too bad, but he could smell burnt fuel. With clenched teeth, he slopped through the damp grass and peered into the driver's window. Empty. He huffed out a breath.

Guy scrubbed a hand over his chin. It was too big a coincidence for this not to be connected to Belle's silence. Not for the first time, it occurred to him that his wife might be in actual danger.

Not stopping to get back in his car, he ran. By the time Guy slid onto the driveway, sirens screamed in the distance. With each thudding step, his heart hammered the inside of his ribs.

Picking up speed, he avoided colliding with the white car by less than a few centimetres and felt his sunglasses slide off and flick onto the gravel. The sirens were louder now, drawing closer. The front door was open.

"Belle?" He grabbed the doorframe and hesitated. "Belle?" His voice was high, matching the siren's pitch.

Rather than running, he stumbled into the house and stood confused and paralysed by panic and indecision. Despite the cold, sweat trickled down his forehead and stung his eyes. On impulse, he darted into the bedroom and almost ran over the heap lying beside the bed.

Brain struggling to keep pace with what his eyes were seeing, he recognised the form as a man. "Arthur?" Guy scanned the room looking for his wife, but saw only the old man.

Crouching, unsure if Arthur was alive, he shook the man's shoulder. "Hey, mate, are you all right?" When there was no response, he leaned closer.

He heard breathing, faint and almost undetectable. Guy swiped at his forehead with his sleeve, the leather smearing the sweat across his face. It was only then that he took in the condition of the bedroom and the knot in his stomach dropped like a dead weight.

Guy left the old man and sprinted through the house, screaming his wife's name. He made it as far as the dining room before he saw that the back door was open and bolted towards it.

At the edge of the deck he spotted the two women near the pool and for a heartbeat, he closed his eyes. The relief was like the warm sun on his skin, washing his face and soothing his soul. Guy jogged the length of the ramp and called out Belle's name.

The two women turned. He didn't recognise the older woman and hardly registered her presence. There was less than a few metres between them, but the look on his wife's face stopped him. It was there, in her eyes, the hurt and the pain. He couldn't hold her gaze. That's when he saw the body in the pool and the strength in his legs ebbed.

Like an old man, he hobbled off the ramp, unable to pull his eyes away from the girl floating in the water. The dark hair, it had to be Katrina. "Who?" He tried to form the question certain that he didn't want to hear the answer. "Is that…?"

There was noise and commotion behind him. Voices and the rattle of trolley wheels. Above the clamour, Belle's voice was clear and strong. "It's the girl you ran over and left on the side of the road."

Chapter Twenty-seven

"Will you come with me?" The trolley bumped over the driveway as the paramedics wheeled Belle towards the waiting ambulance. Ahead of them, Arthur was trundled into a second vehicle, an oxygen mask covering his face. She was being selfish. Joan had been through more than enough already and now Belle wanted more.

Joan, standing back as they loaded Belle into the emergency vehicle, glanced in Guy's direction. "Shouldn't... I mean, don't you want–"

"Please." Belle tried to keep the desperation out of her voice, but she wasn't ready to let Joan go yet. Nor did she want Guy overwhelming her with explanations and apologies.

Guy seemed about to protest, but one of the four police officers who were milling in and out of the house approached him. "Mr Hammer, could I speak to you?"

Guy gave Belle a pleading look then turned to the officer. "It's Mr Stone. Guy Stone. Hammer is my wife's name." It was an explanation she'd heard her husband make on countless occasions only this time his voice was flat, almost robotic.

Joan's hand was bound tightly against her body with thick white bandages and an oversized wax jacket was draped around her shoulders. She gave Belle a brisk nod and allowed one of the paramedics to help her into the ambulance where she sat to Belle's left.

A siren shrilled and both women jumped. "Your friend is in the other ambulance," the young male paramedic explained.

Belle wanted to ask about Arthur but knew the paramedics wouldn't be able to give anything but vague outlines of Arthur's condition. Instead, she closed her eyes and for the first time in days she felt close to calm. What would happen next, she didn't know and, for the time being, didn't care.

* * *

Two days after surgery and three days since almost drowning, two officers sat at Belle's bedside. The room's only window looked out on the river which was grey and churning under stormy July skies.

"My sister went into labour early. Earlier than expected. We, Guy and I, were in Fremantle having dinner. Guy won a bet about the Grand Final and we were celebrating. It was silly really. He only won twenty dollars, but he was so pleased." Belle licked her lips. She intended to tell them everything, even the parts that made her want to crawl into herself like a hermit crab. "I'd been drinking." The younger of the two plain-clothed officers made a note on his pad. She couldn't see what it was.

"I wasn't drunk, but not fit to drive so when the call came from Mark, my brother-in-law, Guy drove us to the hospital."

"And had Mr Stone been drinking?" The older of the two officers, a man in his fifties with closely cropped red hair, asked the questions.

Belle pulled in a breath before answering. "Yes, he'd had a drink with dinner. One, maybe two. I'm not sure."

She had the urge to slip her thumb into her mouth and gnaw at her nail. Instead, she curled her hands into fists. "Anyway, after a few hours we decided that Guy might as well go home. You see, he had an audition coming up and had to catch an early flight the next day."

"What time did your husband leave the hospital?" The redhead, Detective Lowcomb, asked. His voice was calm, patient, as if used to talking about matters that shattered people's lives.

"I'm not sure... Around ten or eleven o'clock." She touched her cheekbone. Her eye, still healing, but mercifully unaffected by the ordeal, was covered with a smaller, nylon patch.

Lowcomb nodded. "And he drove your car..." He hesitated and looked over at his partner who flipped through the pages of his notebook.

"A green 1963 Holden EH sedan." The younger officer supplied the missing information.

"Yes, that's right." Belle had been talking for over an hour, the questions jumping back and forth between her ordeal with Georgia and the night the girl claimed to have been hit by Belle's car. Belle reached out and grabbed a glass of water off the bedside cabinet. Her throat was dry and still bruised from the girl's attack.

"So when Georgia Meadows arrived at your home, you'd never seen her before?"

Belle took a sip of water and winced. "No, never." She tried to keep her tone calm even though she'd answered the same question three times.

"Did you ask to see any ID?" The question came from the younger officer, one of the few times he'd spoken during the interview.

"No. I told you I was expecting a caregiver from Peel Care in Mandurah. My husband had arranged for someone to come and stay while he was overseas. I had no reason to doubt she was who she said she was." She didn't blame the detectives for wanting to go over her story. The things that had happened, the violence and terror, they were difficult for her – although she had lived through them – to fully comprehend. To an outsider, her story would seem convoluted and almost unbelievable.

But she'd agreed to the interview against her doctor's recommendation, because she wanted to tell her story before putting it behind her. Yet, it seemed the telling of it wasn't enough. The police wanted to go over and over the events, making her realise this would not be the only time she would be questioned about Georgia's death.

"All right, Mrs Hammer." Lowcomb gave a tight smile. "I think that's enough for now." He stood and straightened his tie. "I know this has been difficult for you, so I appreciate your willingness to help." He pulled a card out of his back pocket and set it on the bedside cabinet while the younger officer closed his notebook and stood. When he spoke again his tone was softer, less official. "I don't doubt the truth of anything you've said. It's our job to go over the facts. I'm sorry if it seems harsh."

"No, no, I understand." For the last few days, Belle had been swinging from resolute to emotional. The detective's few words of kindness threatened to set off a bout of tears. She clamped her lips together and nodded.

"Okay, well." He jerked his chin towards the card lying on the table beside her. "If you think of anything else, you have my number."

"Yes, thank you. But how is Arthur? Do you know?"

Lowcomb raised his eyebrows and pushed out his lower lip. "I don't really have much information on your neighbour other than that he's in Royal Perth Hospital and in stable condition."

When the officers left, Belle let her head fall back on the pillows and watched a small cabin cruiser battle the rough surface of the Swan River. As painful and protracted as it had been, there was a lightness that came from telling her story.

The door flapped open with a rubber *swish* and Joan's head appeared. "Feeling up to a visit?"

It was the first Belle had seen of her neighbour since they arrived at the A & E department three days ago. Her ruddy cheeks and kind smile were a welcome change after almost an hour and a half with the police. "Joan." She sat forward and motioned to the chair. "I'm so glad you're here."

Joan approached the bed and after a brief hesitation planted a kiss on Belle's forehead. "Sorry I didn't come sooner." She settled herself in the chair Detective Lowcomb had occupied only minutes ago. "But I was told that we weren't to speak until we'd both given statements to the police."

"How was it?" Belle watched the older woman unbutton her coat with one hand then slip it off her shoulders. "I mean talking to the officers."

Joan hooked a strand of hair behind her ear. "Not too bad. They were mostly interested in what I saw out by the pool."

"About that." Belle folded her hands in her lap. "You saved my life." Joan opened her mouth to protest, but Belle held up a hand. "No, you did and I want to thank you. You were there…" She could feel the emotions bubbling up again so she plunged on before she dissolved into tears. "You were there when I thought I was completely alone and… And I'll never be able to thank you enough."

She thought she saw tears shining in Joan's eyes, but the woman lifted her chin and spoke without a quiver. "I knew something was wrong the night before, but like the old woman I am, I dithered. But," she settled her coat over the arm of the chair, "I'm glad I could help. Now, let's talk about your recovery. What are the doctors saying?"

Belle shook her head, but couldn't help smiling. "No. First, how's your hand?"

194

"On the mend." Joan held up her left hand and tapped the metal splints surrounding her pinkie.

"And Arthur?" He'd been on Belle's mind since she'd been admitted, but they were in different hospitals so, apart from what little she'd got out of Lowcomb, all her information came from the news.

"He's doing very well. I saw him this morning. A hairline skull fracture and half a dozen stitches." She frowned. "They suspect he had a mild stroke at some point. His left arm's a little numb, but they're saying that with some physiotherapy he'll regain full use again."

Belle let out a long sigh. "The poor man, what he went through. He... he was trying to help me. My sister's getting me a new phone so I'll be able to call him and thank him soon."

"Yes." Joan ran a hand over her skirt. "He's enjoying the hero treatment the young nurses are lavishing on him. Arthur is quite a resilient man."

Belle thought she heard a note of admiration in the way Joan described their neighbour and stifled a smile. The visit lasted half an hour. Most of that time, at Joan's insistence, was taken up with talking about Belle's knee reconstruction surgery.

Before leaving, Joan pulled a little notebook from her handbag and wrote out two phone numbers: hers and Arthur's. "Now," she said pulling on her coat. "If you need anything, give me a call. I'll drive back into Perth on Friday so I can visit you and swing by and check on Arthur. My car's out of commission so they've given me a zippy little loan car with one of those reversing cameras." She picked up her handbag and slung it over her shoulder. "I'll be glad when you're both home. Despite all the comings and goings of forensic vans, police cars, and news crews, Silver Gum Lane is a lonely place without neighbours."

* * *

After the dinner tray had been collected, Belle's sister stopped in to check on her progress and to deliver the new mobile phone she'd purchased. Bethany, as always, had a great deal to say, but the visit was brief because Jack had a cold and Bethany was eager to get home to her son. Before leaving, she mentioned receiving several calls from Guy.

"He wants you to call him." Her sister hovered at the end of the bed. "I've never really liked him, but he sounds sort of…" Bethany shrugged. Her skin was lightly tanned after two weeks under the Balinese sun. "Sort of broken. What do you want me to tell him?"

Belle felt a surge of weariness and the need to be alone. "Just tell him I need time." Belle rubbed her still bruised cheekbone. "I don't know what else to say."

Bethany squeezed the toes on Belle's uninjured leg. "After what you've been through, the least he can give you is time." Her usually cheerful face was troubled. "I can't believe he…" She held up her finger. "No, I can believe he lied to you. What I can't get my head around is how he could leave that girl in the street and…"

"Please." Belle closed her eyes, realising her voice was too loud. "I don't want to think about it now. I'm just so tired."

Bethany let go of Belle's toes. "You're right. I'm sorry. I didn't mean to upset you." She came around the bed and slipped her arm around Belle's shoulders, pulling her close and kissing the top of her head. For a moment Belle let her weight fall against her sister. A few days ago she didn't think she'd ever see Bethany again. It was good to feel this close to her.

"Okay." Bethany was moving again. "I'll come in tomorrow. Get some sleep."

Alone, staring at the now dark window and watching the city lights across the water, Belle couldn't get her sister's words out of her head. *He sounds sort of broken.* Maybe that made two of them. Only Belle had been broken for a long time. She hadn't really been whole since the day she wandered away from her mother at the department store.

She wanted to put the whole tired mess out of her mind, but every time she closed her eyes she saw a slideshow of horrors: the girl in the boot, Georgia floating face-down in the pool, and her own feet small and encased in red trainers.

Tomorrow, her orthopaedic surgeon wanted her up and walking with a frame. While she dreaded the idea of putting weight on her reconstructed knee, the thought of ever going into another wheelchair sent gooseflesh racing over her arms and neck. It would be a difficult and painful day, but she couldn't get the rest she needed until the last piece of a thirty-five-year-old puzzle was slotted into place.

Belle leaned over and picked up the phone Bethany had left on the bedside cabinet. Her sister had programmed a list of phone numbers in the contacts. She was thoughtful in that way. Belle relied on her younger sister to do the little things she'd never kept track of. That was another reason she had to make the call, to understand why it was her sister she turned to when things were rough.

Belle flicked through the list of names, stopping when she found what she was looking for. The time display above the number showed 7:12 p.m. It would be later in Melbourne, after ten. In many ways, this conversation frightened her as much as all the terrors she'd experienced over the last week. Only this wasn't something that could be surgically fixed.

She screwed up her eyes, willing herself to have the courage to finish what had started so long ago. Not giving herself time to back out, she opened her eyes and made the call. The ringing seemed endless as though there was no one at the other end and just a dark vacuum. A small part of her wanted to hang up and pretend none of it ever happened, but wasn't that what set all this off in the first place? Her ability to turn a blind eye to everything that was wrong with her life?

A voice came on the other end, sleepy and familiar. Belle swallowed. "Hi, Mum. It's Belle."

Chapter Twenty-eight

There was something liberating about being behind the wheel. A feeling that made Belle lower the window and let the spring air fill the car. She'd been driving again for three weeks, but not her old Holden. The vintage car was long sold and replaced by a sleek blue Mazda. The new car handled smoothly as she pulled into the driveway.

Joan's house was more of a cottage, small and painted a serene shade of pale blue. Belle pulled in behind her neighbour's new hatchback and turned off the engine. She enjoyed these lunches. In many ways, they were the highlight of her week. But today would be special, not just because she was off her crutches, but because she had some news to share with her new friends.

Joan greeted her at the door wearing a sensible looking grey skirt and navy jumper. On seeing Belle's new walking cane, her expression morphed from pleased to surprise. "You're off the crutches!" She pulled Belle in for one of her one-armed hugs. "I'm so happy for you." She let Belle go and then ushered her inside.

In the kitchen, Joan busied herself setting the table while Belle set up on a stool at the kitchen bench and chopped continental cucumber for the salad.

"Where's Arthur?" Belle asked and popped a piece of cucumber in her mouth. "Surely we're not having one of our Silver Gum Survivor Group meetings without him." Belle couldn't help chuckling at the name Arthur had given their little group. It was funny, in a grim sort of way. And that's what they were really, the three of them: survivors.

Joan set the cutlery down and came over to stand in front of Belle. "I've asked him to come at one o'clock so we could have some time alone."

Belle stopped what she was doing and regarded her friend. "That sounds serious. Is everything all right?"

"Oh, yes. Everything's fine." Joan leaned against the sink. "I just wanted to ask you something." Joan tucked a strand of grey hair behind her ear. "Well, two things really. There is something else, but it can wait until Arthur gets here."

"Go ahead, ask me anything." Belle was doing her best to keep her tone light, but a sliver of worry was creeping its way down her spine.

Joan nodded, but didn't smile. "Come and sit at the table."

A few minutes later, after making a cup of instant coffee for Belle and tea for herself, Joan joined Belle at the kitchen table. Outside, birds twittered in the trees above an array of spring flowers blooming in Joan's well-ordered garden.

Joan seemed uncharacteristically nervous. "This is going to sound strange, but bear with me." Despite the sun shining through the windows, she cupped her hands around her mug as though she needed warmth. "It's about the night that girl, Georgia, was in your house."

The sliver of worry turned into a cold shiver. Belle didn't like talking about Georgia or anything that happened that night. She opened her mouth to protest, but seeing the intent look on Joan's face, she simply nodded.

"You'll think me crazy, but that night I found a packet of throat lozenges in my glovebox. Larimax Throat

Lozenges to be precise. They were Roger's favourite. Just smelling them was like having him in the car with me." Joan shook her head. "The strange thing is I'd been through that glovebox since he passed away and I swear there were no lozenges in there." She looked into Belle's eyes. "I'd have remembered because... Well, because I missed him so much, I almost bought a packet just to sniff." She gave a humourless laugh.

"Oh, Joan." Belle reached out and touched her friend's hand that was still wrapped around the cup.

"I know. I'm a sentimental old chook."

"No, you're not. You're one of the bravest people I've ever met." It was true. In the days and weeks after Joan had pulled Belle out of that swimming pool, Belle had often caught herself replaying the event and marvelling over the things Joan had done. The things she'd been able to do.

"Well, I don't know about that, but I know those lozenges weren't there before that night. And I think if I hadn't found them, I might not have been brave enough to pay you a second visit." Joan let go of her cup and rubbed her now healed pinkie. "Finding them just when I was feeling so torn and uncertain was one thing, but then, when we got to the hospital and I checked in the pockets of my jacket, they were gone."

As her friend spoke, Belle's mind threw up an image: Joan with her hand bound to her body with white bandages, the jacket over her shoulders as a paramedic helped her into the ambulance. Belle remembered the rush of affection she felt towards the woman – a woman she barely knew, who'd saved her life.

"I just wondered if after you returned home, you might have found them out near the pool." Joan tutted. "I know the police went over the place with a fine-toothed comb so the chances are slim, but I thought I'd ask."

Belle shook her head. "Sorry, no." She wished she could set Joan's mind at rest, but when she finally worked up the courage to go near the pool again there'd been nothing left from that terrible morning.

"Never mind." Joan took a sip of her tea. "I'm sure they blew away or were carried off by a crow. Sorry to make such a fuss."

"Or," Belle said and picked up her own cup, "maybe there are some happenings that go beyond explanation. After all that's happened in my life, I've learned not to discount anything. I believe the world swings in a wide arc, from great good to extreme cruelty. I saw that the morning Georgia tried to kill me. Not everything is as it seems." Now she wasn't just talking about Georgia and the throat lozenges, but Guy and their marriage, her childhood and the reasons why she had felt so distant from her mother, and even the reason she'd turned to alcohol for so much of her adult life.

Joan frowned and for a moment both women were silent. After a few minutes, Joan spoke. "There is something else. Guy..." The name came out in a rush of breath. "It's been almost two months and you haven't talked about him. I don't want to pry, but it worries me."

Belle knew this conversation was coming. She'd had similar ones with her sister over the past months. But the truth was she hadn't been able to bring herself to see her husband. After her statement to the police, Guy was charged with dangerous driving and leaving the scene of an accident. He pled guilty and was due for sentencing in the coming week. Since then he'd sent her begging emails, dozens of them confessing to things she'd always suspected, but again had turned a blind eye to. For a while she hated him, but the feeling didn't last. What she needed now was time. Not to heal, but to harden.

"I'm not ready to see him yet. It's hard to explain, but there's a part of me that wants to pretend none of this happened so I can go back to loving him."

"Is that what you want?" Joan's voice was soft. "Because if it is, no one will think less of you."

Belle knew Joan meant it. Her new friend would support her whatever her decision. Part of her new strength came from having good friends around her. Friends and the whole truth about her life. "Thanks, but I'll think less of me." Belle tipped her head back and looked at the ceiling. "I don't want to go back to the life I had. None of it was real. Guy's not a bad person, he just…" She stopped herself before she could begin making excuses for his shortcomings. She met Joan's gaze and smiled. "The short answer is I won't ever go back to Guy. And, when I'm strong enough, I'll tell him that face-to-face."

"Fair enough." Joan picked up her cup. "I'd better get a wiggle on with this lunch or we'll be eating salad and thin air."

Arthur knocked at the door at exactly one o'clock. When Joan led him into the kitchen, Belle couldn't help comparing the clean-cut man to the rumpled drunk she'd been so afraid of only months before. She suspected his time in hospital gave him a chance to not only heal, but dry out. By the change in his appearance, Belle guessed he was still on the wagon. As always, he brought hand-picked wild freesia for Joan and their sweet fresh smell immediately filled the kitchen.

"How lovely." Joan took the flowers and went in search of a vase.

As she opened and closed cupboards, Arthur sat at the table. "Belle, you're looking well." He nodded at the walking stick leaning against her leg. "Very stylish."

"Thank you." Belle picked up the cane. "I'm quite speedy on this thing. And…" She tapped the end of the sick on the kitchen floor. "It's handy for…" She almost said dance routines, but thinking about dancing brought Georgia to mind and the joke died on her lips.

She could see Arthur waiting, the smile on his face turning into a look of concern. Not wanting to ruin the atmosphere, she forced out a laugh. "For squashing cockroaches."

Arthur grimaced. "In that case, I'm glad we're not eating at your house."

Joan served grilled salmon drizzled with creamy avocado dressing, followed by mango, kiwi and blueberry fruit salad. The lunch was delicious and as always Belle was surprised by how unselfconscious she felt with Joan and Arthur. Maybe it was because they'd seen each other through horrors that most people couldn't imagine. Or maybe they were just a group of people that somehow clicked. Whatever the reason, she felt her life was finally settling into a calmness that had been missing even when she thought she had it all.

"Before we finish..." Belle put down her napkin. "I have some news. Good news, really." Arthur raised his eyebrows in a now familiar gesture as Joan put down her fork. "I've started a new book. Just the outline, but..." She rubbed at her temple. "I think it's coming along."

"I'm so glad to hear it." Arthur rapped on the table with his knuckle. "About time you got back to work."

"Arthur." Joan looked shocked, but Belle could see a smile lifting the edges of her mouth. "That's wonderful news. I can't wait to read it."

After the congratulations had finished, Joan started to rise. "I'll just clear these things away."

"No, Joanie, you've outdone yourself." Arthur placed his hand on Joan's wrist. "You relax. I'll clear away."

Belle noticed Joan's already ruddy cheeks flush a darker shade of pink. For a second, the woman Belle thought was unflappable seemed flustered. "Oh. All right. Thank you." Joan sat back and placed her hands in her lap.

"He's right, Joan." Belle had to work to cover her smile. "Next time lunch is at my house." She raised her voice for Arthur's benefit. "I promise no cockroaches in the food."

As lunch wound up, Belle remembered something Joan said when she first arrived. "You said there was something on your mind, but it could wait until Arthur was here."

"Oh?" Arthur finished stacking the dishes and returned to the table. "Is everything all right, Joanie?" There was real affection in his voice, making Belle wonder if Arthur was developing feelings for Joan that went deeper than friendship. She hoped so – if it made them both happy.

"Yes, everything's fine." She nodded to the empty chair and Arthur took his cue and sat beside her. When he placed his hands on the table, Belle noticed the slight tremor in his left hand.

"I didn't want to bring this up until we'd finished lunch, but I spoke to the Victim's Liaison Officer yesterday."

No one commented, but they all understood what Joan was talking about and the mood shifted from light-hearted to sober. "I wanted to ask about the inquest into Lea Whitehead's…" Joan hesitated as though gathering strength. "Into her murder."

Belle wanted to close her eyes, but knew if she did she'd see the girl in the boot. Lea Whitehead, her body crumpled, a jagged stick protruding from her throat. Their lives were moving forward. Belle's life was beginning to take shape again, but Lea would never realise her future. Of everything that happened, the violent death of the young carer was the hardest to bear.

Joan ran her hand over the placemat in front of her, swiping at unseen crumbs. "It seems the State Coroner is satisfied with the material produced from the investigation into Lea's death and has decided not to hold an inquest. Well, not unless anything new presents itself."

Belle wanted to say something, but all she could summon was relief. Relief at not having to relive the whole ordeal in the Coroner's Court. Relief at not having the details rehashed in the media.

"I see." Arthur seemed unsurprised by the news. "I must say, an inquest didn't seem likely, but it might have helped her parents."

At the mention of Lea's parents, Belle realised how selfish she was being. Maybe an inquest would have been painful for her, but it might have given the girl's parents some closure. She could only imagine how agonising it must be for them to try to come to terms with losing their daughter in such a violent and senseless way. She remembered their grief at the memorial service: raw and shocked. They moved through the ceremony like robots.

"Yes." Joan was looking at Belle now, waiting for her to say something. But when Belle remained silent, Joan continued. "I didn't want to do anything without talking to both of you, but I thought it might be nice to have a bench dedicated to Lea." She shrugged. "Maybe at the walkway on the lake. Somewhere people can sit and enjoy the beauty of this place while still remembering a young woman lost her life. What do you think, Belle?"

For a second she couldn't answer. "Yes. It's a very nice idea."

"Definitely," Arthur added. "A very thoughtful way of remembering her."

"I'll speak to the Victim's Liaison Officer, ask her to speak to Lea's parents and make sure they're happy for us to go ahead." Joan rubbed her pinkie again. "It's not much, but it might help them to know we remember her."

* * *

The afternoon had turned chilly so Belle drove home with the window up. Talking about Lea Whitehead had stirred up memories and with them the familiar impulse to stuff down the painful feelings, to turn a blind eye to the things she didn't want to face. As she rounded the bend and her house came into view, Belle knew she would have to face her demons or fall back into the bottle and drown in them.

The memorial bench was a good place to start. Pulling into the driveway, she decided she would call Joan tomorrow and suggest they pick out the bench and plaque together. After that, she knew there was a long road ahead. At some point she would have to see Guy, then make good on her promise to visit her mother. But, for now she'd start with small steps and, as her mind and body healed, her steps would grow stronger.

The End

If you enjoyed this book, please let others know by leaving a quick review on Amazon. Also, if you spot anything untoward in the paperback, get in touch. We strive for the best quality and appreciate reader feedback.

editor@thebookfolks.com

www.thebookfolks.com

Also by Anna Willett:

BACKWOODS RIPPER
RETRIBUTION RIDGE
UNWELCOME GUESTS
FORGOTTEN CRIMES
CRUELTY'S DAUGHTER
THE WOMAN BEHIND HER

SMALL TOWN NIGHTMARE
COLD VALLEY NIGHTMARE
SAVAGE BAY NIGHTMARE

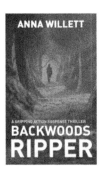

BACKWOODS RIPPER

Paige and her husband are stranded in the outback. He is injured, Paige is pregnant. They have no choice but to seek help from a strange woman who lives in an old hospital. Paige begins to fear for her child.

RETRIBUTION RIDGE

Milly thinks that her sister's invitation to go hiking in the Outback is a chance to heal old wounds. Think again Milly. But what greets them in the wilderness is far more than the humiliation her sister had prepared. It is a confrontation with her worst fears.

UNWELCOME GUESTS

Caitlin seeks to build bridges with her husband after the loss of their baby. Unfortunately, their holiday getaway is not what it seems when they find a man held hostage in the cellar. When the house owner turns up, armed and dangerous, Caitlin will have to quickly decide whom she should trust.

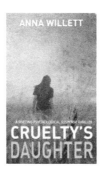

CRUELTY'S DAUGHTER

Mina's father was a brute and a thug. She got over him. Now another man wants to fill his shoes. Can Mina overcome the past and protect herself? 'Cruelty's Daughter' is about a woman who tackles her demons and takes it upon herself to turn the tables on a violent man.

FORGOTTEN CRIMES

A reunion with her friend Rhetty, triggers a series of flashbacks for Gloria of events that occurred four years previously. Rhetty encourages Gloria to revisit the site where a woman died to understand the strange memories. But doing so will put her in danger and force her to confront an awful episode in her past.

THE WOMAN BEHIND HER

When Jackie Winter inherits her aunt's house, she makes a chilling discovery. Worse, she finds that she is being watched. When someone is murdered nearby, she finds herself in the frame. Can she join up the dots and prove her innocence?

SMALL TOWN NIGHTMARE

Lucy's brother is the only close family she has. So, when he goes missing, she begins to panic. She heads out to a rural backwater, Night Town, his last known location, but when she investigates deeper the locals don't respond kindly. What lengths will the townsfolk go to protect their secrets? And how far will she go to protect her kin?

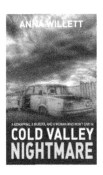

COLD VALLEY NIGHTMARE

Investigative journalist, Lucy, agrees to help look for a child who has gone missing in suspicious circumstances. But in so doing she will have to confront her own feelings of loss and abandonment. When she uncovers a dangerous criminal network, she'll have to draw on all her resolve to escape and see her mission through.

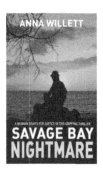

SAVAGE BAY NIGHTMARE

When journalist Lucy Hush's brother is accused of murder, she goes on a desperate search for the truth. But her inquiries are unwelcome and it's not long before she stirs up a vipers' nest full of subterfuge and deceit. Can she get justice for her brother, or will she become another victim?

All of these books are available free with Kindle Unlimited and in paperback from Amazon